"I love you, Matt.

"For what you're doing for me and the baby," Cathie rushed on breathlessly.

Matt understood what she meant but found himself remembering the last time he'd heard those words. They'd come from Cathie then, too. She'd been sixteen.

He'd thrown the words back in her face as if they hadn't meant a thing to him. Love seemed to come so easily to her. It was one of the things that had fascinated the crazy, half-wild boy he used to be.

He wanted to tell her there was nothing to love. That it was all an illusion.

But her words now rolled oddly around inside him, his brain, his chest and the pit of his stomach.

I love you, Matt.

Just words. They'd scared him to death all those years ago. Yet they sounded so different to him now….

Dear Reader,

Welcome to more juicy reads from Silhouette Special Edition. I'd like to highlight Silhouette veteran and RITA® Award finalist Teresa Hill, who has written over ten Silhouette books under the pseudonym Sally Tyler Hayes. Her second story for us, *Heard It Through the Grapevine,* has all the ingredients for a fast-paced read—marriage of convenience, a pregnant preacher's daughter and a handsome hero to save the day. Teresa Hill writes, "I love this heroine because she takes a tremendous leap of faith. She hopes that her love will break down the hero's walls, and she never holds back." Don't miss this touching story!

USA TODAY bestselling and award-winning author Susan Mallery returns to her popular miniseries HOMETOWN HEARTBREAKERS with *One in a Million.* Here, a sassy single mom falls for a drop-dead-gorgeous FBI agent, but sets a few ground rules—a little romance, no strings attached. Of course, we know rules are meant to be broken! Victoria Pade delights us with *The Baby Surprise,* the last in her BABY TIMES THREE miniseries, in which a confirmed bachelor discovers he may be a father. With encouragement from a beautiful heroine, he feels ready to be a parent…and a husband.

The next book in Laurie Paige's SEVEN DEVILS miniseries, *The One and Only* features a desirable medical assistant with a secret past who snags the attention of a very charming doctor. Judith Lyons brings us *Alaskan Nights,* which involves two opposites who find each other irritating, yet totally irresistible! Can these two survive a little engine trouble in the wilderness? In *A Mother's Secret,* Pat Warren tells of a mother in search of her secret child and the discovery of the man of her dreams.

This month is all about love against the odds and finding that special someone when you least expect it. As you lounge in your favorite chair, lose yourself in one of these gems!

Sincerely,

Karen Taylor Richman
Senior Editor

Please address questions and book requests to:
Silhouette Reader Service
U.S.: 3010 Walden Ave., P.O. Box 1325, Buffalo, NY 14269
Canadian: P.O. Box 609, Fort Erie, Ont. L2A 5X3

Heard It Through the Grapevine

TERESA HILL

SPECIAL EDITION™

Published by Silhouette Books

America's Publisher of Contemporary Romance

To everyone at St. Mary's and all of our friends
in Greenville, South Carolina.

Thanks for making our ten years there wonderful.

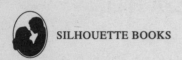 SILHOUETTE BOOKS

ISBN 0-373-24546-7

HEARD IT THROUGH THE GRAPEVINE

Copyright © 2003 by Teresa Hill

This edition published by arrangement with Harlequin Books S.A.

Visit Silhouette at www.eHarlequin.com

Printed in U.S.A.

Books by Teresa Hill

Silhouette Special Edition

Heard It Through the Grapevine #1546

Other books written under the name Sally Tyler Hayes:

Silhouette Special Edition

Magic in a Jelly Jar #1390

Silhouette Intimate Moments

Whose Child is This? #439
Dixon's Bluff #485
Days Gone By #549
Not His Wife #611
Our Child? #671
Homecoming #700
Temporary Family #738
Second Father #753
Wife, Mother…Lover? #818
*Dangerous To Love #903
*Spies, Lies and Lovers #940
*Cinderella and the Spy #1001
*Her Secret Guardian #1012

*Division One

TERESA HILL

lives in South Carolina with her husband, son and daughter. A former journalist for a South Carolina newspaper, she fondly remembers that her decision to write and explore the frontiers of romance came at about the same time she discovered, in junior high, that she'd never be able to join the crew of the *U.S.S. Enterprise.*

Happy and proud to be a stay-home mom, she is thrilled to be living her lifelong dream of writing romances.

The Little Dipper

Polaris

Cassiepeta

The Big Dipper

Emma's Stars

Chapter One

The stick turned blue.

Cathie Baldwin sank down to the floor of her tiny bathroom. Taking stock of her situation as objectively as possible, she decided she'd never been this afraid, this upset or this ashamed of herself.

She was twenty-three, certainly old enough to know better, and they'd been careful, darn it. So careful.

Of course, as mothers had no doubt been telling their daughters for decades, the only truly safe sex was no sex at all. Which was what she'd had for years. *No Sex.* She'd waited so long, and now that she'd finally found someone she'd thought was special enough to share her bed…now this.

She looked at the test stick again, just to be sure. If anything, it looked bluer than before.

Fine. Tears welled up in her eyes, and she let them fall.

No one had ever cried forever, had they?

She feared she might set a record in the event. *Olympic Gold, Longest Crying Jag in History,* Laura Catherine Baldwin, the preacher's daughter. The good girl. Pregnant college dropout who horrified her father's entire congregation, shamed her parents, infuriated her four overgrown, overprotective brothers, shocked a dozen aunts, uncles and cousins too numerous to count and generally messed up her life.

And her baby's.

Oh, God, she was going to have a baby.

Cathie thought she was about as miserable as she could be.

Then the lights went out. Everything in the apartment whined down and stopped. The heat, the refrigerator, the computer. Everything.

She whimpered. Honestly, she was the most pitiful thing. On the way to the kitchen, she cracked her toe on the corner of the coffee table, swore softly as she hopped the rest of the way, her toe throbbing.

In the kitchen, she found the big pillar candle on the counter by the coffeepot. But the matches proved stubbornly elusive. She was feeling along the top of the refrigerator when, just as she thought she found them, her hand hit something else.

It rumbled and rolled on top of the fridge, and the next thing she knew, came flying down and hit her on the forehead.

"Ouch." She put her hand on her poor head for a moment, then reached up and, finally finding the matches, struck one and lit the candle.

Her first stop after that was the little mirror hanging in the hallway, to check the damage. She had a red splotch on her right temple to match her tear-reddened eyes.

She was headed back into the kitchen to see what had hit her when hot wax from the candle dripped onto her hand.

"Ouch!" For a second, she thought she'd caught her pajama top on fire, that she was cursed for sure. Then the lights decided to come back on.

She groaned, blew out the candle, wiped the dot of hot wax off her hand, and then looked down at the mess she'd made of her own floor.

That's when she saw the little wooden box in the corner by the trash can.

Cathie frowned at it.

Granted, it had been a really lousy day and maybe she was closer to hysterics than she realized.

Because it seemed a lot like God had just hit her on the head.

Warily, she crept over to the little wooden box as if it might have sprouted wings and flown into her forehead, all on its own. But she'd knocked it off the refrigerator.

That was all.

No big mystery there. No odd powers at work.

She felt silly for still having the thing.

It was her God Box. One of the quaint traditions of her father's church. A turn-it-over-to-God thing. All the kids got one. For problems they didn't think they could deal with on their own. Cathie had taken an introductory psych class, so she understood the concept. Letting go of things we simply can't control or change.

They had a saying in her family: *Take it to the Box.*

She'd done that with so many problems over the years, some of which had been solved and some she was still hoping to see resolved. They were still in the Box, scribbled on little slips of paper.

At least, they had been inside, until she'd knocked the Box off the refrigerator.

Feeling foolish, she got down on her hands and knees, scrambling to find those little papers and stuffing them back inside, as if any of those childhood secrets and wishes mattered now.

Her life had been so much simpler then.

Cathie sat on the floor, glancing warily at the Box, feeling too guilty and too ashamed of herself to say a prayer.

But it wasn't so hard to say, *Help me, please.*

Or to write it down.

It felt silly, but she'd been crying forever, no closer to an answer than she had been when the blasted stick had turned blue. She could use all the help she could get.

Scribbling frantically through fresh tears, she managed to get down one frantic plea, then folded the paper up into tinier and tinier pieces, like she had when she was little. She tucked the paper inside and was just starting to think, *Okay, what do I do now?*

Honestly, it hadn't been a minute.

When her doorbell rang, she was as startled as she'd been when the Box hit her on the head.

Not a single interior light was visible through the windows of the shabby, old house perched on the edge of the North Carolina college campus.

The house's paint was flaking, the yard needed

mowing, and the police should probably be called to deal with the two men half a block away, guzzling beer, shoving each other and swearing. A cat was on the prowl for its dinner, garbage was piling up on the curb and there didn't seem to be a functioning street-light on the whole block.

Matthew Monroe climbed out of his very expensive, steel-gray Mercedes and frowned. What the hell, he thought, activating the car's security system. No reason to make it easy. Things had been much simpler in his car-thieving days.

Pocketing the car keys, he frowned as he headed for the old house, the last place in the world he wanted to be tonight or any other night.

Because *she* lived here.

But Mary Baldwin was the closest thing Matt had ever had to a mother, and Mary was worried about her daughter. Which meant someone had to go see if Mary's little girl was all right. Matt was the closest thing to family Cathie had in town, so he was elected.

He climbed the front steps and pounded on the flimsy, pressed-wood door. An odd sensation—faintly reminiscent of nerves—rumbled around in the pit of his stomach. Nothing really worried him, anymore. *Except her.*

He waited, not hearing a sound. But her ancient Volkswagen bug was parked out front.

Saturday night, he remembered. She could be out on a date. It was amazing, really. Cathie Baldwin, all grown up. *Dating.*

He swore at the image that brought to mind. A hot, summer night. No moon, but a million stars. Cathie, barely sixteen years old, jailbait if he ever saw it. With tears in her eyes, a flush of embarrassment in her cheeks and indecent amounts of pale, creamy soft skin bared for him to see.

Everything had been fine between them until that night. Cathie had been a scrawny little kid who'd once devoted herself to saving his worthless hide. He'd lived in her parents' home from the time he was fifteen until he was eighteen, a part of them but not really one of the family, a distinction he'd always understood.

Even once he was eighteen and no longer a subject of the state's foster care program, Mary, a do-gooder of the highest order, and Cathie kept treating him like family. During his breaks from college, Mary hounded him until he finally gave in and found himself back in the midst of the Baldwin clan once or twice a year.

It had been one of those visits, when he was twenty-three, that Cathie had thrown herself at him. As Matt saw it, he owed the Baldwins, and if it was the only decent thing he ever did in his life, he was going to keep his hands off their daughter.

He'd been doing fine until eight months ago when Cathie finally left home for college and ended up here in his town. Cathie, indulged and protected her entire life, who might as well walk around with a sign that said Take Advantage of Me. She'd always believed there was good in everyone. Even snipping, snarling, wild-eyed, would-be teenage car thieves.

One last time, he pounded on her door.

Finally, he heard the faint sound of footsteps coming from inside. A voice sounding oddly strained, called out, ''Who's there?''

''It's Matt,'' he admitted, though it certainly

wouldn't make her want to open the door. Silence. Matt grew more uneasy. "Cath? You okay?"

"I've got a cold. I don't think you want to catch this."

"I'll risk it. Open up."

"Matt, really. I'm fine. I was just sleeping, and I want to go back to bed."

He pushed an impatient hand through his hair, then shoved the hand into the pocket of his slacks. Cathie Baldwin in a bed?

No, he would not go there.

"Cathie, I've been thinking this door really is too flimsy. I should replace it with something stronger." He'd done all the locks when she'd moved in, but that didn't seem like enough now. "So breaking down the door wouldn't bother me at all."

"You wouldn't."

"Try me," he shot back, unleashing every bit of worry he'd had over her safety in those two little words.

The door cracked open. Through the narrow opening, he peered into the darkness and saw nothing more than the outline of her face.

"It's pitch-black in there," he complained.

"I told you I was sleeping. And now you've seen me. You can go."

"Me? Or your mother, Cath? Take your pick, but one of us is going to be inside that apartment, if not tonight, tomorrow."

"You wouldn't."

"We've been through this already with the door. You know I would."

She fumbled with the chain lock and finally stepped back to let him inside.

He looked her over from head to toe. She angled her face away from him, hiding behind a curtain of light brown hair sprinkled with blond sunshine. It was the beginning of December, but unseasonably warm. She had on a big sweatshirt in Carolina blue, the color of one of the local college sports teams, and a ragged pair of faded blue jean shorts. He couldn't quite make himself stop staring at the lean expanse of skin, from her thighs all the way down to bare feet and dainty, pink-tinted toenails.

Damn. Matt tugged at his tie, then reached for the tiny lamp on the table in the corner and flicked it on.

Cathie winced at the flood of light and quickly turned away. "I suppose if you're staying, I could at least offer you some coffee."

She headed for the kitchen. She hadn't made it far when he caught her by the arm and spun her around. Flicking on the overhead light, he saw that her eyes were puffy and red, her face pale, a trail of tears on her cheeks.

Irritation gave way to fury at anyone who dared hurt her. He'd always been protective of her. It had been there right from the beginning, when he was fifteen and she was eight, with pigtails, gaps in her teeth and skinned knees, an optimist to the core, forced to endure both the pampering and the supreme torture of being the youngest and the only daughter in a family of four boys.

So what the hell were her brothers doing, scattering themselves from one end of the earth to the other, when she needed someone? It was all too easy, staring at her poor, sad face, to imagine the myriad of ways in which a young woman alone in a strange town could be hurt.

"Why don't you tell me what's upset you," he said in a tightly controlled voice.

She stood there trying in vain to hide her feelings. *Give it up, Cath,* he thought. She'd always been so easy to read.

"Come on. Tell me," he said softly, for a minute finding and slipping into that old, easy manner between them from the days when she'd been his champion, the one who could always be counted on to take his side in anything and seemed absolutely determined to draw him into the world of her big, boisterous, affectionate, nosy family. Where he would never belong. He'd never belong anywhere. It had always been so clear to him. Why she didn't see it, he'd never understand.

"Matt, please," she pleaded, her eyes big and wide and blue, swimming in moisture, her lashes spiked together.

Even in the woman, there were the best qualities of the little girl. She could totally disarm him with nothing but a look in her eyes.

"Please what?" he said, caught, unable to walk away.

"Please leave it alone."

"Can't do it." Matt suffered from an unfortunate, long-standing urge to touch her, even in the smallest, most inconsequential of ways. Though he certainly knew better, he reached for her. Her lashes fluttered down as the pad of his thumb brushed across one of her wet eyelids, and then the other.

It was so nice to touch her.

Matt dried her tears as best he could with the back of his hand. Pale and utterly still, Cathie stood there, not even breathing, her lips slightly parted, her cheeks pale and damp.

She looked like she had that long-ago night. Heart-broken and very, very sweet. Another memory he'd tried hard to forget rushed to the surface. The feel of her lips pressed to his, of sweet, impossibly shy kisses, innocence so pure it was hard to imagine in the world he knew. She'd gotten him into the back of a pickup in a secluded valley on her parents' farm, taking him completely by surprise, absolutely convinced that she was in love with him and that they belonged together.

He'd had a hard time convincing her they didn't and had gotten the hell away from her as fast as he could. Okay, *almost* as fast as he could. He was a man, after all, and she'd practically laid herself bare on a platter in front of him. She'd been embarrassed and hurt. He'd been gruff and insulting, because she'd scared him half to death because of the way she'd tasted, the way she'd felt beneath him and the way he'd wanted her.

Should have gone to jail fifteen years ago, he thought soberly.

"What's gotten you so upset that you're sitting in the dark crying your eyes out?" he asked.

"There…uh," Cathie stumbled over the words. "There's nothing you can do, Matt. Nothing anyone can do."

He held his breath as he asked, "Are you sick?"

"No."

He swore softly. For a minute, crazy things had

gone through his head. That she was dying. That he might never see her smiling face again. Never hear her laugh.

Of course, she wasn't dying. She was just making him crazy, as usual.

"Not sick? Okay. What else? Flunking out of school?"

"No."

That was highly unlikely, given the fact that she'd worked so hard to get here. Her father had fallen ill with a heart condition during her senior year of high school. His heart transplant had nearly wiped out the family financially. All of her brothers had been either in college or committed to the military, and Matt knew they'd helped out monetarily, as much as they could. But Cathie had been the only one left at home. The years she'd normally have spent in college, she'd spent helping her mother care for her father, helping run the family bed-and-breakfast, taking courses at the local community college when she could.

He knew it was still a struggle financially and held out a brief hope that this could be about money. "Need me to loan you fifty bucks until payday?"

"No," she insisted. "It's nothing like that."

"Okay. You want to play Twenty Questions? I'll play."

"Matt, please, just go," she said, with that quality in her voice that always had him wanting to give her anything in this world. Except this.

"Sorry, but you're a mess, Cath. You need somebody, and in case you haven't noticed, I'm the only one here."

"This isn't your problem," she argued.

"Your mother made it my problem, and you know the way she works. If she doesn't hear from me soon, she'll call and ask how you are, and I'm not going to lie to her. I'll tell her you're a wreck, that you wouldn't tell me anything, and the next thing you know, she'll be pounding on your door. Is that what you want?"

"No," she insisted. "I just need some time to figure everything out. Could you just go away and give me some time?"

It was an entirely reasonable request, and hard as it was to believe, she was an adult. But he'd didn't think he'd ever seen Cathie looking so fragile or so hurt. He doubted he could have walked away from her now if his life depended on it.

"Sorry. Can't do it. Tell me what's wrong."

She eased to the right, her hip resting against the kitchen counter, which put her face fully into the light for the first time. It looked like she'd been crying for hours. A white-hot anger simmered in his gut, and he knew he'd been asking the wrong question. Not *what* was wrong with her, but *who?* Who had done this to her?

"This is about a guy, isn't it?" Looking utterly miserable, Cathie let her gaze meet his for a second. She blinked back fresh tears and looked away. "Want me to go beat him up?"

"It wouldn't help."

"I could call all of your brothers and the five of us could have at him."

"My brothers would kill him."

"That depends," he said quietly. "What did this guy do to you?"

Cathie didn't say anything. He was afraid she was crying again. Matt was considering his options when something on the kitchen counter caught his eye.

It was a small, rectangular box. Not able to believe what he was seeing, he swept past her and picked it up.

It was one of those home pregnancy tests.

In Cathie's kitchen?

He turned to look at her. Really look. In his eyes, she'd hardly changed since that night when she was sixteen. So it always surprised him when he saw evidence that she had indeed grown up. He ran the numbers in his head. Her eight, to his fifteen. Her sixteen, to his wise-in-the-ways-of-the-world twenty-three. He was thirty now, which meant she was twenty-three.

Matt had a bad habit of still thinking of her as sixteen. This was Cathie Baldwin, after all. The good girl whose life could not have been more different from his. Matt's hard-living, hard-drinking, never-met-a-fight-he-didn't-like father had died when Matt was barely old enough to remember him. His mother had taken it badly, which to her meant drowning her sorrows in a bottle, too.

Matt ran wild, eventually living on the streets, headed for disaster, when he bungled the theft of Cathie's mother's car. For reasons he would never understand, rather than let him go to jail, the Baldwins had offered to take him into their home, something that had surely saved his worthless hide. Matt would not repay a debt like that by lusting after the Baldwins' only daughter.

Besides, he'd always known what life had in store for her. A nice guy. A really nice one. Respectable.

Wholesome. Not a single skeleton in his closet. Not a single arrest. Someone from a good family. Not necessarily well-to-do, but kind, God-loving people. She'd have a nice little house in the mountains her family called home, teach Sunday school and raise a half-dozen kids, and she'd be happy and well-protected her whole life.

But it hadn't worked out that way. Another man had slept with her. Carelessly? Casually? Thoughtlessly? And that man had either failed to take the time to protect her or hadn't cared enough to do so.

Matt held the proof in his hand.

He crushed the box of the home pregnancy test in his hand, taking out a mere shred of his anger on it, then threw it across the room.

Cathie winced as the box skittered across the floor, then opened a drawer and pulled out a white, plastic stick-like thing. "I'll save you the trouble of asking. The stick turned blue."

Blue? he thought numbly. "Blue's bad?"

She nodded hopelessly. "If you're not finished with college, not married, don't have a lot of money and your father happens to be a minister, then…yes, blue's bad."

Chapter Two

Cathie stood there waiting for him to say something, still hardly able to believe he was here.

One minute, she'd been staring guiltily at the Box and the next, the doorbell had rung. She'd hastily shoved the Box in a drawer, and there was Matt. As if she'd conjured him up out of thin air. As if she'd asked, and the man upstairs had chosen to deliver Matt.

Cathie fought the urge to go stare up into the sky and say, *Excuse me? What is he doing here?*

Obviously, someone had gotten their wires crossed.

Matt didn't even want to be in the same room with her.

All because she'd fallen for him ages ago and then thrown herself at him, when he didn't want her at all. Which was just about the stupidest thing a woman could do.

Okay, not as stupid as getting pregnant when she hadn't finished college and wasn't married. But that night with Matt ranked right up there on her list of all-time stupid moves. She hadn't wanted to come here to college because he lived in the same town. But the university had offered her the best financial aid package, and she'd needed all the help she could get.

Cathie hadn't chased after him in years, but darned if she didn't still compare every man she'd ever met to him. Even Tim. If she was honest, she'd admit that Tim reminded her the least little bit of Matt.

"So," Matt said finally. "What are you going to do?"

"I don't know," Cathie, the girl who always had a plan, said. "I just found out, and I'm still trying to make myself believe that it's real. That it's happening to me."

"Do you want to marry this guy?" he asked.

"I don't know." Though it would make her humiliation complete, she admitted, "I'm not sure it matters. I'm afraid he won't want to marry me."

Beside her, Matt stiffened, a mixture of disbelief, surprise and then anger washing across his face. For a minute, she thought he was going to ask the same question she'd been asking herself in the hours since the stick turned blue. Why in the world was she sleeping with a man who wouldn't marry her if she was pregnant with his child?

"He's…uh." She closed her eyes and forced herself to start again. "He's been different the last few weeks. A little…distant, maybe? Distracted. Impatient."

Through clenched teeth, Matt said, "Why?"

"I don't know." Around the same time she noted

subtle changes in her body that warned her something was wrong, she'd discovered an alarming number of doubts about Tim.

Matt, the tough guy of old wrapped in a thousand-dollar suit and still looking only faintly civilized, said, "Do you want me to talk to this guy for you?"

"You're starting to sound like one of my brothers again."

He swore softly. "I'm not one of your brothers."

"I know." She risked another glance in his direction. When she was a little girl, she'd look at him and think he was a wild thing she was going to tame. Like a pup who'd been kicked too many times, always waiting on someone to turn on him.

Cathie had followed him everywhere when he'd first come to live with her parents. She'd watched him with a kind of fascination as he warily watched her in return. She'd smile and he'd frown. She'd laugh and he'd put that same scowl on his face she'd seen tonight, the one that said she was getting to him.

Closing her eyes, she let herself remember, just a bit, her and Matt together. *God,* she thought breathlessly, *how she'd missed that boy.* Of course, God already knew. She'd certainly told him often enough, back in the days when she was trying to talk him into bringing Matt back to her. She hadn't done that in years and fought the urge to pull out her Box and say very emphatically that he was not what she had in mind when she asked for help.

Still, she missed him so much, the lost boy who'd become her best friend. She'd seen more of him tonight than she had in years.

For just a moment, she let herself imagine a wild-eyed black knight coming to her rescue, making everything right somehow.

"What?" Matt growled, staring at her through midnight-colored eyes.

She shook her head and tried to smile, feeling hopelessly sentimental about a relationship she feared meant next to nothing to him. She, on the other hand, needed nothing more than the slightest touch of his fingertips to her cheek to know that she was every bit as attracted to the man as she'd once been to the boy. The awful part was that neither the boy nor the man had wanted her.

And now she feared she was in the same shape—no, worse—with another man she feared wouldn't want her or her baby. Obviously, there was a pattern here she should probably figure out, so she didn't keep repeating this same mistake.

"Cathie—"

"Sorry. I was just thinking. And wondering…why did you come here tonight?"

"I wasn't going to," he said. "Mary asked me to come by tomorrow, but I had a meeting tonight. When I got done, I wasn't too far from here, and…I don't know. Something just told me this might be a problem that shouldn't wait. Why?"

She frowned. *Something just told him?*

"No reason," she lied. No way she was explaining what she'd done to him.

"Cathie, why don't you let me talk to this guy for you?"

Sure. He and Tim could compare notes. *Why didn't you want Cathie? Really? Me, either.* She groaned, feeling sick suddenly and swayed on her feet.

"Easy." Matt's hand shot out to grab her. "I've got you. Need to sit?"

She nodded, letting herself lean on him as he steered her to the sofa.

"Better?" he asked once she was sitting.

"Yes. Thank you." She had to get him out of here. Fast. He'd seen enough of this little drama that was her life. "And I appreciate the offer, about Tim, but I have to tell him myself. And my mother. My brothers. My father. They're going to be so disappointed. Matt, I don't think I've ever disappointed them. My father counsels teenagers at the community center on being responsible and careful. How is it going to look when his own daughter ends up pregnant and all alone? And to his congregation? I know some of them will give him grief over this. Plus his heart is…I don't know. He hasn't admitted it to me, but something's going on. He was so sick before. We almost lost him. I don't want him worrying over me, and for this, he'll worry night and day."

Utterly miserable, she stared up at Matt. He couldn't have surprised her more when he sat down beside her and put his arm along the back of the sofa, motioning her closer. "C'mere, Cath."

She hesitated, knowing she should not let herself get too close. But she needed him so badly right now. "Just for a minute?"

"Whatever it takes," he said, his gaze steady and sure.

Cathie let herself lean against him a little, slipping progressively closer until her face was buried in the warm curve of his shoulder and his arms were clamped tightly around her. A long, deep shiver ran through her—her last-ditch effort at control. And then she was lost, just melting into the heat and the rock-solid strength of him.

With her face pressed against his neck, with every breath she took, she inhaled a bit more of the essence of him—something dark and dangerous and, after all these years, blessedly familiar. One of his hands stroked her hair tenderly. The other gently kneaded the knot of tension at the base of her spine. She gave up any hope of holding her tears in any longer. He pulled her closer and held on tighter, as if he might be able to hold her tightly enough to stop her body from trembling so badly.

"It's going to be okay," he whispered.

She didn't believe that, but it was nice to have him hold her this way. She stayed there for the longest time, feeling safe and not so very hopeless. When she lifted her head, she found his face only inches from hers.

Deep, blue eyes, so familiar and flecked with gold, stared down at her, his jaw set in a grim line. His hair was shorter than it had been as a teenager, but still as dark, and, if anything, his body was even leaner and more powerful. It was so easy to find herself caught up in that old familiar spell that was Matt.

His hand settled against the side of her face. Carefully, gently, he wiped the tears from her cheeks in a touch that was so sweet, so tender.

Just for a moment, something flared in his eyes. If he'd been any other man, she would have sworn he was about to kiss her—the way a man kisses a woman he desires. And then, as she watched, the look drained away. Every little spark simply disappeared.

Unnerved, Cathie pulled away. Because she wasn't sure her legs could hold her, she didn't even try to stand. Instead, she scrambled to the opposite end of the couch. Drawing her knees up to her chest and wrapping her arms around her legs, she watched him as he watched her.

There were new lines of tension at the corners of those beautiful eyes of his, not even a hint of a smile on his lips. But she could say with absolute certainty that he was every bit as gorgeous at thirty as he had been at fifteen, nineteen, twenty-one, twenty-seven. Not that it mattered. He was simply being kind to her, and she was carrying another man's child.

"I'm sorry," she said finally.

"It's all right," he insisted. "Look, Cathie, there's no place I have to be tonight. I could stay a while."

"Thanks, but I have to make some decisions, and I have to talk to Tim."

"All right." Looking uncharacteristically uncertain, he stood up and headed for the door. "If you need anything…" he said roughly.

And then Cathie couldn't even look him in the eye anymore. If she did, she'd take him up on his offer and ask him to stay. She felt like such a fool.

"I really don't want to leave you like this," Matt said, sounding like her prickly lost boy, put out with her but, at the same time, still trying to take care of her.

"I'll be fine. I'm going to go to bed and hope I can figure some things out in the morning."

"Okay. I'll stall if your mother calls."

"Please. I'll call her tomorrow. Or I'll go see her and Dad."

With the front door open, he hesitated once again. "Cathie, anything. I mean that." Matt squeezed her hand one last time, released it, then turned and disappeared into the night.

He was almost home when the phone in his car rang. He snatched it up, thinking Cathie might be calling. "Hello."

"Matt? Hi. This is Mary. I'm sorry to bother you, dear, and I know you think I'm just a silly old woman who's much too protective of her daughter...."

"You've always been a bother," he said, trying to make light of this while he decided how much to tell her. "But I don't think you're silly, and you'll never be old."

"Thank you, dear. I notice you have the tact not to mention my overprotectiveness, and I appreciate that. I don't suppose you know how my girl is?"

He closed his eyes and wrestled with his conscience. Cathie had a right to explain herself when she was ready. Still, Matt genuinely liked Mary Baldwin, and he didn't want to lie to her.

"I saw her, and you're right. She has some things on her mind right now."

"Things she can't talk about with her own mother? Matt, is she in trouble?"

"She has some decisions to make, and I'm sure she's going to talk to you about this, as soon as she figures it out for herself. Mary, please don't ask me for any more."

Mary let out a long, slow breath. "Maybe I should drive down there tonight."

That would work. Especially if it meant Cathie

didn't end up in his arms again. That had been sheer impulse, one that came from his time with the Baldwins. They were a family of touchers. Bear hugs. Kisses. Arms around each other's shoulders. It was as natural to them as it was for Matt to hold himself apart from everyone. They seemed to have latched on to him in a way he just didn't understand, and they'd never truly let go. They'd take care of Cathie now.

Still, she'd asked for his help, and he'd promised to try to stall.

"Mary, it's late," he reasoned. "Cathie said she'd call you tomorrow, and I told her if she needs anything from me, all she has to do is call."

"Thank you, dear. If she had to be so far away from home, I feel better knowing you're close by."

Not close enough, he thought, feeling guilty that he'd kept his distance while some jerk was taking advantage of her. "She's special, Mary."

"I know, dear. She's a wonderful girl, and I'm very proud of her. Still, I can't help but worry. She's always been too trusting for her own good."

"Yes, she is." That had to be the problem. She'd trusted the wrong man.

"Matt, we miss you, too. Christmas is coming. All the boys are going to be home this year, and we'd love to have you. And don't tell me you're too busy. You have to take some time off every now and then."

Matt shook his head. No surprise here that Mary would go from mothering Cathie to trying to mother him. No one had ever really done that for him, except Mary. His own mother and father had gotten together when they were far too young, a quick, stormy relationship that had burned out long before Matt had come along. His father liked to go out and have a good time. He drank too much and got into arguments he tended to settle with his fists, or something worse. His mother drank to forget everything, including Matt. He'd been more of a hassle to her than anything else. By the time he was eight, he was roaming the streets, taking care of himself. By the time he was thirteen, he was living on those same streets after his mother kicked him out.

Not that any of that mattered anymore.

"I am planning some time away from the office," he admitted. Honestly, he couldn't remember where he decided to go. He recalled pointing to something from an array of brochures and leaving the details to his travel agent.

"Christmas is a time for family," Mary argued. "Promise me you'll think about coming here?"

"All right." He'd think about it. He just wouldn't go.

"You can't run from us forever. Sooner or later you're going to come home."

"Mary—" he began.

"I'll be waiting for your call. Bye, Matt."

With that, she was gone, still able to outmaneuver him as neatly as always. He remembered standing in her kitchen his first morning there, cussing like a sailor, thinking to shock her, to make her turn her back on him, as everyone else had.

He soon learned that Mary didn't shock easily, and she didn't get flustered, no matter how filthy his language was. She'd used the same tone with him fifteen years ago, kindhearted, a bit bossy, but polite, as if he'd shown her the same courtesy she showed him.

Then she'd smiled and proceeded to steamroll right over him, quietly making her wishes known, until somehow he'd decided he'd be better off doing what she suggested in the first place.

If that tactic didn't work, shame did. She could make him feel like dirt without so much as lifting a finger. It was all in her eyes and the tone of her voice. No matter what he did wrong, she'd find out eventually. And she'd be hurt, as if she'd somehow failed him and not the other way around. She'd look at him and he could all but hear the words going through her head. *What am I going to do with you, Matt? What have I done wrong that I can't reach you?*

Before long, she'd become his conscience. Even if he didn't care what happened to himself, Mary did. Matt didn't want to disappoint her. It became a litmus test for him. *If I do this, what's Mary going to think? What's she going to say?*

For the first time, he stopped to think before he shot off his mouth or let fly with his fists. With Mary on one side of him and Cathie on the other, he hadn't stood a chance. Before they were done, he'd taken a long, hard look at himself and his life, figured out that there comes a time when it doesn't really matter how screwed up anyone's parents were. Maybe the world had dealt him a lousy hand, but lots of kids grew up without anyone who gave a damn about them. In the end, it was what he chose to do with his life that counted. Once he realized that, Matt had done surprisingly well for himself. He had a gift for numbers, something Cathie's father had picked up on right away, and they'd no doubt called in some favors to get him admitted to the university here and to help get him a scholarship.

He had more money than he knew what to do with now, a company of his own that specialized in providing security for financial transactions over the Internet, a huge house, a car that positively reeked of money. He worked hard, and played just as hard when the notion struck him, which it seldom did.

He still couldn't lie to himself well enough to say he was happy. It had all failed to satisfy him for some reason.

Matt eased back into the soft leather seat of his car and stared into the night.

As always, when he arrived at home, the place was dark and silent. He didn't really want to go inside, which was ridiculous given what he'd paid for the place. It was too big for him and had never felt like a home. Tonight, it seemed worse than usual. Because his mind was on another house, an old one in the mountains, crammed to the rafters with people and laughter. With a sense of permanence. Of family.

Matt still remembered how it felt, living in the midst of the Baldwin clan. Their house had never been quiet or empty.

Shoving the memories aside, he pulled the car into the garage and walked into the kitchen, losing his keys, his wallet and his tie as he went. Upstairs in his bedroom, he kicked off his shoes and started working on the buttons of his shirt, the eerie quiet getting louder and louder with every passing minute.

Maybe what he needed was a woman. Someone to come home to, to fill the empty rooms and chase away the silence.

Glancing across the room at the big, wide bed, he imagined her waiting there for him on the nights when he came home really late. She'd have pillows propped against the headboard, one small light burning on the bedside table, a book in her lap.

Her hair would be long and loose, the light from the lamp glinting off of it. In his mind's eye, he could see it so clearly, the image as enticing as any dream he'd ever had.

The woman lifted her head, smiled at him and held out her arms to him.

Cathie, he realized.

He was thinking of Cathie in his bed.

Matt knew what he had to do. He had to help her and then forget about her. He sure wasn't letting her anywhere near his bed, even in his imagination.

There had to be a way to help.

It turned out to be so simple, he couldn't believe it took him so long.

Money.

He had plenty, and she didn't. She'd have doctor bills, tuition, child care, rent, utilities, diapers, all kinds of stuff. He wanted her out of that lousy neighborhood, too. Matt could do all that. She wouldn't like it, but he simply wouldn't take no for an answer this time. If her father hadn't refused his help when Jim Baldwin had been so ill, Cathie would have finished college by now and maybe even been married. A baby wouldn't have been a problem.

Matt was back on her doorstep shortly after eight the next morning, telling himself money was the answer. It was easy, too. He could write a check. He wouldn't even have to see her again. *Money*. He was excited for the first time in years that he had so much of it.

Cathie opened the door wearing a pair of pale yellow, cottony pajamas. "Hi."

She looked soft and rumpled, cold and dangerously touchable. Her hair was loose and falling around her shoulders, her eyes puffy and red and sad, and it seemed she'd come straight from her bed. He stared. She folded her arms across her breasts, as if to hide herself as best she could. He really had to stop thinking about her this way.

"When I heard the knock, I was sure my mother was here," she said, stepping back to let him inside.

"I stalled as best I could, but it's not going to work for long."

"So, she's on her way? Or is she waiting for you to report back to her?"

"She's supposed to wait for you to call, but you know your mother."

Matt wanted to know what her boyfriend said when she'd told him the news, wanted to know if she'd come to any decisions. But she looked like a stiff breeze could knock her over this morning, and he didn't want to push.

"Have you had anything to eat?"

"No," she admitted, wrapping herself up in a sweater that was thrown over the back of the sofa.

Good, he thought. *Cover up.*

"We could go get some breakfast," he suggested. Get out of this apartment. Go somewhere they wouldn't be alone.

"Matt, you don't have to do this," she said, a hurt

look in her eyes that always managed to cut him to pieces. "I mean, I know my mother harasses you until you show up here."

"She has. But she's not the reason I'm here right now."

Cathie frowned. He thought they were probably going to argue some more about his motives, when all he wanted was to keep her from kicking him out and to find out what that idiot who'd gotten her pregnant had said.

"Come on. I'm here. I'm hungry. You're awake now. You've got to eat. I could cook something while you grab a shower and get dressed."

Please, he thought, seeing bare feet and delicate pink-tinted toenails, *get dressed.*

She didn't move. He could hear the faint sound of her breathing. Finally, she said, "You don't even like me anymore."

"Cathie." He closed his eyes, simply unable to take the hurt he saw in her face. "I have never disliked you. Never even come close."

Tears were glistening in her eyes the next time he looked up, and he wasn't sure she believed him. "You thought I was a pest. You always did."

"You were a pest." He laughed, couldn't hold it in. The memories were too strong. "You absolutely baffled me. Why in the world would a little girl like you give a damn about me? If you had any sense at all, you would have been scared of me and stayed away. Hell, if your whole family had any sense, they would have never let me inside your house."

"You didn't turn out so bad," she said softly.

"Neither did you, Cath. Honestly, I never disliked

you. Can you trust me about that, at least?'' She considered him warily from across the room. ''Humor me, okay? Get dressed. Let me feed you. Then, if you still want me out of here, I'll go.''

''Promise?''

He frowned. ''Do I have to promise?''

''Matt!''

''Okay.'' That was a lie. He felt absolutely no guilt in telling it, not now that she needed him. It had always been her and her family doing so much for him, and him thinking he had nothing to give them in return.

Not that he'd ever have wished a situation like this on her. But still, the situation was what it was. She needed help, and he could give it to her.

''I know it's hard,'' he said. ''To be in trouble and let someone help you. I've always wondered—why'd you do that for me? Why didn't you give up on me and leave me alone?''

''I just couldn't.''

He nodded, understanding exactly. ''Do me a favor, Cath. Don't make it as hard for me to help you as I made it for you to help me.''

She was quiet for a long time. It left him feeling edgy, like he might just do something crazy before he got out of here. She'd always made him a little crazy.

''Why did you come here this morning?'' she asked finally.

Neatly trapped and unwilling to lie about this, he confessed. ''I came to offer you money.''

She looked hurt. ''It's not that simple.''

''I know.'' Too late, he saw that writing a check just wasn't going to cut it.

Chapter Three

Cathie hid in her bathroom for what had to be the longest shower on record, finally emerging in a cloud of steam. In her tiny bedroom, she tugged on a pair of jeans and a white blouse. While she was buttoning her blouse, she found herself staring at the Box, which now sat on her dresser.

What is he doing here?

She'd slept with her arms wrapped around that Box, filled with so many little slips of paper with his name on them. Maybe someone had gotten confused again. Cathie's handwriting had always been atrocious. Maybe she had a guardian angel who needed glasses or something.

The Matt notes are old notes. I don't worry about him that much anymore. I try not to even think about him.

The Box remained stoically silent, reverently housing all her secret hopes and dreams, including one, new, desperate plea she'd written that morning, right before he'd shown up, again.

I asked for help. Not him. He's fine now. Okay, maybe not fine. I'm afraid he's lonely, and that he'll never really let anyone love him. But he's not miserable. He always wanted money and a nice house of his own. I know all that really means to him is a sense of security, which he never had before, but he's got all that now.

Of course, she didn't think those things made a person particularly happy. They would help her, in the shape she was in, but she didn't think happiness was found in a big bank account and a nice house. Matt loved his work. She knew he was well-respected and keenly intelligent, and having people recognize those things meant something to him. If she ever asked for anything else for Matt, it would be that he let down his guard enough to let someone love him, but she wasn't sure if he had it in him to love someone back. He'd always held himself apart from everyone else. Those were walls she feared would never come down.

She glanced back at the box, because there wasn't anyone else to talk to at the moment. *What do I do now?*

If she'd expected a lightning bolt or a booming voice coming out of nowhere, it didn't happen.

She just kept getting Matt at her door.

She supposed she had to go out there and let him make whatever offer he wanted, while she tried not to argue. He was right—he had made it terribly hard for her to help him, fighting all the way and nearly frustrating her to death. So, she would try not to do that to him. She'd try to just take what he offered, if her pride would let her.

Cathie found him in the kitchen wielding a knife covered with peanut butter. He'd made toast with peanut butter and jam.

"Wasn't much to choose from," he said. "And I knew you liked this."

She'd made it for him ages ago. It had been one of her favorite treats as a child, and it sounded pretty good to her now. Bland, but filling.

"Thanks," she said, having learned the hard way that she did not want to let her stomach stay empty for long, even if she didn't feel like eating.

She sat down and nibbled gingerly. Matt sat and watched her.

"Better?" he asked, when she pushed her plate away.

"Yes."

"So, you saw the guy?"

"Talked to him. He's, uh…away for the weekend." That's what she'd believed. She'd never even doubted it. Was he such a good liar? Or was she just a fool? "Let's just say I can't believe I was that stupid."

"Oh, Cathie. I'm sorry. He's an ass. Lots of men are."

She nodded, still having trouble believing how wrong she was. "He seemed so charming, and he was good-looking and all grown-up and sounded so sincere, and I fell for it completely. I believed everything he said, and he didn't mean any of it."

"And the baby? Is this boy—"

"He's not a boy, Matt. He's a grown man. One of my professors, actually."

He swore roundly.

"It gets worse." Cathie turned away, as angry at herself as she was at Tim. "He's, uh…he's married. I didn't know. I swear. I never would have had anything to do with him, if I'd known. I guess they've been having some problems and were separated. Or maybe that was a lie, too. I don't know. It doesn't matter, anyway. She's been away, but she's back now and wants to get back together. He offered me money, Matt. To have an abortion. I couldn't do that."

"Okay. Forget about him. The guy doesn't deserve you or your baby."

"I know."

None of which changed the fact that she was going to have the man's baby.

Cathie cleared the table and started cleaning the tiny kitchen, just to have something to do. It was so horrible. She was so ashamed.

"So, what are you going to do?" Matt asked finally, when she couldn't find anything else to do to keep her from facing him.

"Have a baby, I guess."

"And then what, Cathie?"

"I don't know."

A part of her wanted to run home to her mother and father, but she was about to become a mother herself. Surely that meant she couldn't go running home to her own mom and dad, expecting them to fix everything.

"I'm really worried about my father," she admitted. "He's had a lot of medical tests lately, and no one's saying why. But I know that means something's up.

With transplants, there are so many things that can go wrong, even after all this time. We're not supposed to worry him, and he's going to be so worried. I love him so much, and I'm afraid of what this might do to him, Matt.''

"Yeah, he's going to worry. What about school? How much do you have left?''

"Year and a half. If I'm lucky, I might make it through spring semester, which would only leave a year, but still...'' A whole year left, with a brand-new baby. "I think I really should consider giving this baby up for adoption.''

"Could you do it?''

"I don't know. But there are people who can't have children any other way, nice people who love each other and are married and have good jobs. I'm barely getting by. School is so expensive, and if I quit before I graduate, what kind of job will I be able to get? How could I take care of myself and a baby like that?''

"Cathie, I know you. If you give up this child, you'll regret it for the rest of your life. This would break your heart.''

"I know," she cried. "But what else am I going to do?''

"Let's deal with one thing at a time, okay? You want to keep this baby, right?''

"Yes," she whispered. It was a part of her, and as upset as she was at the timing, she'd always known she wanted to be a mother. Her own mother had told her quite seriously that having children was both the hardest thing she'd ever done and the greatest joy of her life.

"You need to finish school," Matt said. "But that

all takes time and money. Time won't be easy to come by with a baby, but money helps there, too, and let's take money off the table right now, okay? It's silly to let that stand in your way when I have more than I'll ever need, and I'd give you anything you need.''

''Matt—''

''It's mostly because of your family that I have what I do today. Don't tell me I don't get to give something back now,'' he insisted. ''Your father's always talking about that, isn't he? Giving something back?''

She nodded. He had her there.

''So, this is how I get to give you back a little of what your family gave me.''

''Okay, but still—''

''I'm not done. You're worried that this will bring a lot of stress to your father and put his health in danger?''

''Yes.''

''What else?'' he asked.

''I'm worried about this baby growing up without a father.''

''You don't know this baby won't have a father. You could find someone you love, someone you trust, and marry him. He could be a great father to this baby. And even if you were married right now, it's no guarantee that you always would be. The guy could walk away. He could get hit by a bus. Anything could happen.''

''I'm still worried. Your father was never around, right?''

''Right.''

''And how was that?''

''It wasn't that unusual where I came from. I mean,

it's definitely not the best of circumstances, but lots of kids don't have fathers.''

''You never knew him?''

''Barely. He died when I was four or five. Got into a fight in a bar. Just a stupid, little thing, but then he was always into some kind of trouble like that.''

''Matt—''

''It's nothing to me,'' he insisted.

''A father shouldn't be nothing to his child.''

''No, he shouldn't.''

''Do you ever hear from your mother?''

''Sure. Any time she needs money. She saw something in the paper about my company a year and a half ago and came running with her hand out.''

''Were she and your father married?''

''No.''

''So…did the other kids give you a hard time about that? Did they call you…''

''A bastard?'' He grinned and shook his head. ''I've been called every name in the book, but not necessarily because my parents never married.''

''Still, it's a big, bad world out there.''

''Yeah,'' he admitted. ''Look, I don't know how things are these days, with so many single parents and divorced parents and all that, but twenty-five years ago when I was old enough to hear it and to ask what it meant, it wasn't a lot of fun the first time it happened. But it's far from being the worst thing life ever threw at me.''

''So, that's not a big consideration, I guess.''

''Well, not necessarily. You'd feel better if you were married?''

''Of course.''

He nodded. "And your father wouldn't worry so much."

"No, but that's not going to happen. Tim's not going to marry me—"

"I wasn't talking about that jerk." He took her hand and held on tight. "Oh, hell, I was thinking... Look, I know it sounds crazy, but...I was talking about me. I think you should marry me, Cathie."

She gaped at him. "You?"

He nodded. "For the baby."

Cathie's heart lurched painfully. *For the baby.* Of course. She tried not to let him see how this both touched her and hurt her, tried to keep it light. "That would be a bit drastic, don't you think?"

"Give it a minute. It could work," he claimed. "We could get married right away. Everyone would assume I was the father of your baby. For all intents and purposes, I would be."

"What?"

"You want this baby to have a name, don't you? You don't want that jerk of a professor of yours to ever have anything to do with your baby."

"No, I don't."

"I have a big house," Matt went on. "There's more than enough room for you and the baby. There's a housekeeper who comes in twice a week, a sweet old grandmotherly type. We'll have her come full-time to help with the baby while you're in class. I know you want to finish school. You'll have to, if you're going to get back on your feet after this baby comes."

Cathie stood there mutely. Matt had actually asked her to marry him. She used to dream that he would, but never like this.

"Your parents would buy it," he went on. "You've been here since May. Your mother's kept sending me over here to check on you, so they know we've been spending time together. We'll tell her we wanted to keep this just between the two of us until we were sure about our feelings."

"I can't lie to them like that, Matt," she said, struggling for any reason she could give him to stop this insanity.

"Will we have to? If we just call them and tell them we're getting married, they'll make all the logical assumptions."

They would. Her parents would never expect her to marry for anything less than love. Still, to tell them she and Matt loved each other, to let them think it...

"It would still be a lie, Matt."

Oh, please. Let it be a lie. Let her remember all the reasons she couldn't love him.

Matt's hand came up to the side of her face, so gently she thought she must be imagining this. He'd never touched her anymore. She closed her eyes, savoring the feel of his touch, as he let his hand linger against her cheek.

"We were good together once, Cathie. Everything was so easy between us. We were the best of friends. Remember?"

"Of course, I remember," she cried. "You're the one who forgot."

He shook his head sadly. The tips of his fingers spread into her hair, his thumb brushing away her tears.

"I didn't forget," he said, his gaze locked on hers. "Cathie, you've always been special to me. I care about you. I always have. I'm not going to lie and say I love you, because you know it's not that. But I do care, and I want to help.''

"I know, but…marriage—"

"It doesn't have to mean anything," he said. "At least nothing more than we want it to mean."

She closed her eyes and hung her head down low. Matt's hand was still on her face, and she felt him ease closer. Gently, he pressed her face against his shoulder and his arms came around her. He stroked her hair, whispered reassurances in her ear, while she wished with every bit of her heart that he could have loved her, just a little.

He was different now. The cool, remote man who'd slipped in and out of her life over the years had been so different from the utterly compelling one who'd shown up at her apartment twice in the last twelve hours. The one who held her in his arms while she cried, offering tantalizing glimpses of the man she always knew he could be.

"Think about all your family's done for me," he said. "It's a debt I never thought I'd be able to repay."

"Oh." Of course. This was something he understood, something he believed in. Never take anything from anyone, unless you absolutely couldn't help it. And if you did, find a way to pay it back. "Matt, my parents helped you because they wanted to, because they came to think of you as part of the family, and families take care of each other."

"Fine, I'm family, and you're in trouble. Let me help you," he said, looking more determined than she'd ever seen him. "Think about the baby, Cath. I want your baby to have everything."

"Everything you never had?" she suggested. "Is that why you're doing this?"

"What if it is?" he said. "Look, I'll be whatever you want mc to be to your baby. I'll be a name on a piece of paper. Someone you share a house with for a few years. Someone who sees your kid every other weekend and on major holidays. Whatever you want, Cathie, I'll do it."

"I don't have any doubts about that." Not for a second. He would take good care of her baby.

Cathie let out a long, slow breath. Last night, when she'd closed her eyes and tried to figure out what she should do, she kept imagining having her baby, handing it over to someone else and watching them walk away with her baby. The baby was crying, and Cathie was crying as well.

But now she saw Matt, her baby cradled tenderly in his arms.

Cathie's heart started to thud in a hard, heavy rhythm. Hope warred equally with the urge to protect herself from him and everything she'd ever wanted, not just from him but *for* him. He needed someone to show him love was real and precious, worth fighting for, worth believing in. Maybe she wasn't that person, but what if her baby was? What if that was the key to his heart?

Cathie's mother always said babies were magical creatures, so innocent, so trusting, so accepting, that they could work miracles.

She could try to explain to Matt that he desperately needed someone to love, that his life wouldn't be complete without it. She believed there was love inside of him, waiting for that one person who could draw it out. And her baby...

Maybe he could love her baby.

Maybe she did have something to give him, after all.

"Look, if it makes you feel any better, we can put a time limit on it," he suggested. "Three years, Cath. Your parents gave me three years. Think where you and your baby could be in three years."

That was Matt, practical to the end. If she'd had any illusions it might be something more...

Still, the situation was what it was. She was pregnant, and he was making her a very generous offer. In three years, she could have her degree and a teaching job. She'd have a two-year-old she could put in day-care, if she had to. Not the kind of life she'd imagined, but a lot more than she'd thought she'd have last night.

"Then what?" she said carefully. "We'd just walk away from each other?"

"Sure."

He probably believed that. That they could live together for three years, and then just walk away from each other. Was she crazy to think he might feel differently before those three years were up?

"Cathie, you're making this more complicated than it has to be. All we have to do is make it through the ceremony without your family getting too suspicious. Then we come back here, move you into my house and get on with our lives. You can go to school. I'll go to work. You'll have your baby. And when this marriage has served its purpose, we'll end it. That's it."

Oh, he did need someone to love. He needed it desperately. Who'd give that to him? Who would he ever let close enough, if not her and her baby?

Matt took her chin in his hand and tilted her face to his. "Marry me, Cathie."

Her breath caught in her throat, because he was so close, so solidly reassuring, so sincere. She opened her mouth to object one more time.

Matt pressed the pad of his thumb to her lips. "I'll take good care of you and the baby. I promise."

Her eyes filled with tears that spilled over and ran down her cheeks. "I know you will."

Cathie felt the ache deep inside her give way. All of a sudden, the tightness was gone. A feeling of peace came over her. She knew she could safely entrust her life and her baby's to Matt. Her heart might well be another matter, because she was going to lose it once more to him, if she hadn't already, just by being here with him and seeing him again.

He had to quit hiding the kind, tender man he could be.

In the end, it was something her father told her that made up her mind.

Her father saw an order and a purpose to everything. He believed people's lives fit together in exactly the way they were meant to. And then he threw in a little of the philosophy of Mick Jagger and the Rolling Stones. That you didn't always get what you wanted, but sometimes, you got exactly what you needed.

Cathie had said a lot of prayers in the last twenty-four hours. There'd been a time when she'd tearfully offered up endless, rambling prayers on Matt's behalf.

Maybe this was her answer to all of them.

"You're sure?" she said, giving him one last chance to back down.

"I'm sure." He smiled, the reckless bad-boy smile of his youth. "Say yes, Cathie."

She closed her eyes and whispered, "Yes."

Matt fastened his strong arms around her and held her close. "Everything's going to be okay," he promised.

And in that instant, Cathie believed him.

She was trembling, so he held on to her for a while. He could take care of her now. Buy her a decent car, and see that she had the best medical care for her and the baby, and that she didn't have to work for a while. Maybe when they separated, he could find a way to talk her into letting him support her and the baby afterward. He'd never miss a dime of the money, and he liked the idea of her and the baby having it.

Yeah, he'd do that, when the time came.

First, he had to make sure she didn't back out on the wedding.

"We need to tell your parents," he said.

She eased out of his arms and looked a little panicked. "I will."

"No. Now. We don't have any time to waste, do we?" he asked, glancing pointedly at her midsection. It was hard to imagine Cathie growing big and round with a baby. And then he remembered something. "Christmas is only three weeks away. We can use that as our excuse."

"Excuse?"

"For getting married so quickly." She gave a little squeak of distress. "It's all right. It's not like we're going to have a big wedding. And we can't spend six months planning it, right?''

''No, we can't. But—''

''Your mother said all of your brothers are supposed to make it home this year, and you'd want to have all of them there, if you were getting married for real, right?''

''Yes.''

''We have to make this look real, Cath,'' he said softly, fighting the urge to push even harder. Once she told her parents, that was it. There'd be no backing out. Picking up the cordless phone on the table by the sofa, he said, ''Call.''

She looked kind of pitiful, like she might cry some more. ''I hate lying to them.''

''It's not a lie,'' he insisted.

The voice of Mary Baldwin rose up inside him. She would definitely think omitting several pertinent facts constituted a lie. He wondered how well she would take the idea of him marrying her daughter.

Matt dialed the number and held out the phone to Cathie.

''I can't,'' she said, shaking again. ''You do it.''

He pulled her against his side, so she wouldn't run away, as Mary came on the line. It was a good thing one of them could tell not-quite-lies so well. That skill was going to come in handy before they were done. ''Hello, Mary.''

''Matt? I hope you have some news for me. How's my girl?''

Here we go. No time like the present. ''She's fine, but she's going to be my girl. I finally talked her into marrying me.''

No lie there. It had taken a great deal of talking to convince her.

"What?"

"You heard me. She's going to marry me."

There were shrieks from the other end of the phone, then tears, then laugher. He'd forgotten how loud the Baldwins could be when they were happy. Before long, Cathie's parents were both on the line. They didn't offer a single objection to entrusting their only daughter to Matt, much to his surprise. They welcomed him warmly back into the family, claiming that in their eyes, he'd always been one of them. They'd just make it official now.

"Matt, I need a moment alone on the phone with my little girl, if you don't mind," Mary said. "Especially if we're going to pull off a wedding in three weeks!"

Matt handed over the phone. Cathie pulled her knees to her chest and the phone to her ear.

"Yes," she said. "If Daddy performs the service, Brett can walk me down the aisle... I love Grandma's wedding dress. It's perfect... Whatever decorations are put up for Christmas at the church will be fine. It's one less thing to worry about... No, just a small thing at home afterward. We just want everyone there."

She was doing fine. She and Mary would have to work so hard to pull off the wedding so quickly, Mary would hardly have time to ask questions.

And then he heard Mary's voice say, "You love him, don't you?"

Oh, hell.

The whole plan would fall apart. Cathie wouldn't lie about a thing like that.

It got quiet for a minute. He wished he'd taken more time to convince her this was the right thing to do and that it was no big deal. Hell, the house was so big and he worked such crazy hours, he'd hardly ever see her and the baby. And his debt to the Baldwins would be paid.

Cathie looked up at him like he was the only solid thing in her world at the moment. She put a hand to her still-flat stomach, and he held his breath, waiting to hear what she'd say. If she'd just think of the promises he'd made her. He'd meant every one of them. He would be here for her and her baby, no matter what. They could make this work.

You love him, don't you?

"I do," Cathie whispered.

Matt nodded, telling her with his eyes that it was the right thing to do, and then he could breathe again, hadn't even been aware that he'd stopped. Life was so strange sometimes.

A moment later, the conversation was over. Matt took the phone from Cathie's trembling hand and put it back on the table at his side, then faced Cathie again. "You okay?"

"My mother asked me if I loved you, and I told her that I do. For what you're doing," she rushed on breathlessly. "For me and the baby. I do love you."

"I know."

He understood exactly what she meant, but found himself remembering the last time he'd heard those words. They'd come from her then, too. She'd been sixteen and mad as hell.

I love you, Matt.

He'd thrown it back in her face, as if the words

hadn't meant a thing to him, as if she didn't, either. She'd been wrong, of course. Not that it was so surprising she might think she loved him. She loved so many people. Everyone. Nearly everything. She was extravagant with it, as if there was an abundance of it inside of her, and it was nothing to add one more person to the list of those she loved.

It seemed to come so easily to her, too. *Love.* It was one of the things about her that had fascinated the crazy, half-wild boy he used to be.

He'd always thought she was begging to get hurt, by loving so easily and so generously. Which, no doubt, was what had happened. She'd fallen for some guy who was completely undeserving of her. It still made him furious, just thinking about it.

He wanted to tell her there was nothing to love. That it was all an illusion, bound to do nothing but hurt her even more, if she persisted in believing in it still.

But her words rolled around oddly inside his body, rattling around his brain, floating around in his chest and the pit of his stomach.

Just words.

They'd scared him so much all those years ago, and somehow sounded so good to him now.

Chapter Four

Matt reverted back to form so quickly and so completely, Cathie thought she might have dreamt that crazy twenty-four hours in which he'd magically appeared in response to her hastily scribbled prayer, heard all her secrets, then talked her into marrying him.

If not for the phone calls from her mother as they planned a wedding—hers and Matt's—for the day after Christmas, she wouldn't have believed it actually happened.

Matt became the polished, confident businessman once again, orchestrating their marriage as he might a business deal. Cathie talked to his secretary as often as she spoke to him, and when she did, he was fast-talking, making decisions in a split second, trying to pay for everything and handle everything.

He arranged to have her things moved into his house after the wedding, wanted her to have an entirely new wardrobe, which seemed ridiculous until he pointed out that it couldn't look like he wasn't providing for *his wife.* She swallowed her pride and spent his money as sparingly as possible, so that if she needed to look like Mrs. Matthew Monroe on occasion, she could do it without embarrassing him.

Matt insisted that she see an obstetrician, the best in town, a woman who came highly recommended by three of his female staff members.

He drove her to the appointment himself—the only time she saw him in that three weeks—and played the attentive husband-to-be perfectly. She tried not to catch her breath every time he got too close, tried not to let those old dreams of her and Matt, together and in love, seep back into her head. How would she be able to breathe once they got married and he was nearby all the time?

The doctor was friendly and thorough. Alone in the exam room with her, Cathie asked for an AIDS test and one for sexually transmitted diseases. A man had gotten her pregnant, after all. She had to consider he might have given her something else, too. The doctor merely nodded, promising to call with the results. She said the baby was just fine and calculated Cathie's due date as July 15.

Matt wanted her to see his house, had offered to let her make any changes she wanted, but the house was the last thing on her mind.

She had to figure out what she was going to do. Try to slip into his life as unobtrusively as possible? Be grateful for what he was doing and for the fact that she'd be able to keep her baby? Or go for broke? Open up her heart and her life completely to him, in hopes he might love her back?

He made it sound like they were going to do nothing but share his house and his checkbook. Like he wasn't the same man who'd held her so tenderly and made her all those beautiful promises about taking care of her and her baby, saving her in a way that humbled her and had given her all those crazy ideas that maybe…just maybe…he could love her.

Was she going to marry the man who'd been so kind and so gentle with her, or the completely self-contained businessman who'd swear he didn't need anyone?

She feared it would be the latter.

That was the one who showed up three weeks later to drive her to her parents' house for the wedding. Matt, all slick and polished, as calm and sure of himself as ever, driving that pricey, steel-gray sports car of his.

She had so many doubts she thought she might drown in them.

Matt carried her bags to the car and opened the passenger side door for her. She stood by the car door, gazing back at the tired-looking, old house she'd called home for the brief time she'd been here, wondering where she'd be three years from now and if she had the courage to take this leap of faith.

"You can't change your mind now," Matt said softly.

"I know." But a smart woman would still try to protect her heart.

Cathie got in the car, trying not to look back anymore. Matt knelt down in the open door of the car and said, "I won't let you down, Cathie. I'll do everything I promised."

And her silly heart started thumping like crazy. There was *that man* again.

"I know you will," she said.

But what if she asked him for more? What if she found the courage? Would it be like that awful time when she was sixteen and had thrown herself at him?

"You don't look so sure, Cath."

"Just nervous."

"About seeing everyone? About making them believe this is real?"

"About everything," she confessed, and thought he was going to take her in his arms again. That would be nice. Maybe she wouldn't cry or forget to breathe, and then she could just enjoy the feeling of having his arms around her.

Nothing felt like being in Matt's arms.

She dared a glance at his face. He might have turned to stone, right there hunkered down in the doorway of the car. Finally, he said, "It's the right thing to do."

That was the businessman talking. The one who drove a status symbol, probably lived in one, as well. Couldn't she just have her teenage car thief back? She'd understood him so much better and known how to handle him.

"Just keep thinking about the baby," he said.

"Okay." That helped. "I'll always be grateful to you for this."

"And don't thank me again," he said, giving her a warning look.

She fell silent. He stood up, came around to the

driver's side of the car, and off they went. They made it out of the city and onto the interstate, heading west toward the mountains, before he said anything else.

"All we have to do is get through Christmas and the wedding. It's three days. Then we can live our own lives," he said. "Your parents will come to visit every now and then. Your brothers might show up from time to time, but that's it. No one else is going to put this marriage under a microscope and try to analyze it or judge it. We get through these three days, and we have nothing to worry about."

"You're right. It's just…it's not going to be easy. They'll expect certain things from us…."

They'd expect her to be in love with him. How hard would that be? All she'd have to do was drop her guard and let all those old feelings show through. But at the same time, she had other secrets to hold inside. The fact that she was pregnant. That the baby wasn't Matt's, and that her marriage was intended to be nothing but a sham.

How was she going to manage that?

"Cathie, we're talking about your family at Christmas and on the day you get married. It's going to be pure chaos. A dozen people dropping by to see you and your brothers and your parents. Everyone talking at once, pulling us in six different directions and probably not giving us a moment's peace. It's a perfect setup for us."

"You're right." Maybe they could pull it off. And then they'd be married. Oh, boy.

"Try to relax." Matt punched a few buttons, turning up the heat, bringing soft, soothing music from the CD player. He grabbed his overcoat from the back seat and put it over her. "Or maybe try to get some sleep. It's going to be a long three days."

So, he was going to take care of her? That would be nice. And familiar. When she was a little girl, pestering him shamelessly and leaving him wanting nothing more than to get away, he'd still been the first person to come running if she ever got into trouble or got hurt.

She was starting to worry that it wasn't fair to him, to marry him letting him think this was going to be nothing but a sham when she wanted so much more. That was about as dishonest as a woman could get, wasn't it?

Or was this the chance she'd always wanted with him? One for him to have all the things he so desperately needed. She wasn't sure if he'd ever loved anyone in his whole life, and he wasn't going to start now, not on his own. She doubted he was even looking for anything like love, and his life seemed so empty to her.

But it was his life, and he claimed to like it just fine.

Who was she to turn it upside down? Or to claim she wanted one thing from him, when she wanted something else completely?

"You're worrying again," he said.

"Sorry. Are you sure this is what you want to do?" *There.* She just said it.

"Cathie, the whole thing was my idea. I'm sure."

"It may not turn out the way we planned," she tried. "I mean, life would be so much simpler if things just worked out the way we expected them to."

"What do you expect to happen, Cathie?"

"I don't know. Things have a way of getting complicated." She thought about saying she didn't want to hurt him, but he'd think that was ridiculous. He was like the man of steel, couldn't be hurt. The man without a heart. So her heart was the only one at risk, right?

She just didn't know.

He took her cold hand in his warm one. "Cathie, just let me take care of things for a while, okay?"

"I'm trying to." She closed her eyes, trying not to think too much about what was right and what was wrong, trying to just be grateful to him for giving her and her baby this chance.

She slept, waking when they were only five minutes from her home.

"Matt!" she complained.

"What? You wanted more time to be nervous?"

"No."

He grinned. "That's what you would have done, and you know it."

She might have begged him to stop, told him it was all a big mistake, that they couldn't go through with this. As it was, she didn't have time to do anything. They pulled up to the house. Someone must have been watching for them, because people started spilling out. Everyone was talking at once. There were hugs and kisses and more tears. Matt got pulled one way, and she was dragged another.

Her mother and her aunts wanted to go over every detail of the wedding, until her head was spinning. Sprinkled into that conversation came questions about her and Matt, about how secretive they'd been and how despite that, no one was really surprised. Had she been that transparent in her feelings for him? She supposed she had and didn't want to think of what everyone was telling Matt.

They all finally came together hours later in the family room, around a roaring fire and a beautifully decorated tree. Her mother passed out glasses of champagne punch, and her father stepped into the middle of the group to offer up a toast.

"In case any of you haven't heard, we have a wedding to celebrate. I'm trying to tell myself I'm not losing a daughter. That I'm just gaining a son-in-law, but…" He looked right at Matt. "She'll always be my little girl."

"I know," Matt said, slipping his arm around Cathie.

"You'd better take good care of her, son."

"I will," Matt promised solemnly.

"Or else," one of her brother's shouted from the side of the room, the other three chiming in with good-natured warnings of their own.

Matt gave her the barest hint of a kiss on her lips. They touched their glasses together, and she pretended to take a sip, while the room exploded into another round of congratulations and laughter.

They all attended an eight o'clock service Christmas Eve. Her father talked about the blessings for which he was so grateful—one of which was being able to officiate at her wedding in two days—and mentioned many other people in the congregation who'd been blessed in one way or another in the past year.

It was a close-knit community. The people truly

cared about each other, in good times and in bad. All those connections were what made life bearable and joyous and fulfilling, her father said. Cathie wondered if Matt, who sat by her side, believed any of those things. If there was anyone who was particularly close to him these days, wishing for his sake that there was. She wanted him to be happy.

Which reminded her. She hadn't even asked if there was a woman in his life.

Cathie groaned at the entirely obvious omission.

"You okay?" Matt, who sat by her side, asked.

"Yes. I just thought of something we forgot."

"What?"

"Later," she whispered. "When we're alone."

It took some doing to arrange that. Late that night at the house, they slipped out the back door into the cold. Snow had fallen earlier in the week and still blanketed the ground. The mountains were a purplish-black in the distance, blending into the night sky.

Matt put his jacket around her and said, "What's wrong?"

"This is...I feel so stupid. I didn't even ask—"

"Ask what?"

"If there was someone else. A woman, I mean. In your life. Now." He got quiet. The look on his face told her there was. "Oh, Matt. I'm so sorry."

"Cathie, it's nothing. She's nothing to me."

"But you were...together?" *Sleeping together?*

"It was nothing, and now it's over."

Which meant, they *had* been sleeping together. She closed her eyes and asked, "What did you tell her?"

"That I was getting married."

"Oh." And she'd just accepted that? That Matt

would go from sharing her bed to marrying someone else so quickly? Cathie didn't want to think about that, either.

"She and I didn't make any promises to each other, Cathie, but you and I did. Which reminds me…" He reached into his pocket and pulled out a tiny, prettily wrapped box. "I was going to put this under the tree for you, but…well, this is probably not the kind of thing people usually do in front of an audience."

"Oh, Matt." She wanted to say he didn't have to do that, but she supposed he did, to keep up appearances and everything. Oddly, no one here had even asked about a ring, and it had been one detail she'd forgotten all about.

"Go ahead," he said. "Open it."

She did, finding an exquisite diamond inside. Square-cut, large and flawless, it rested on a band of intricately carved platinum in a swirling pattern, old-fashioned, like something out of the forties. Like her grandmother's, which was impossible because she'd never taken it off in her life and had asked to be buried with it. Cathie had always loved her ring.

"I asked Mary if she had an idea of what you'd like. She had a photo and remembered your grandmother's had come from a place here in town. The same family still owns the store. They were excited about the idea of trying to copy the old design," he said, taking it out of the box and putting the ring on her finger.

Which was why no one had asked. They'd all been in on the secret.

The ring looked exactly like one she'd dreamed a

man she'd marry would someday slip on her finger. Matt would tell her to keep it when she walked away from him in three years. She could just hear him now saying it didn't mean a thing. What was he going to do with a ring, anyway?

Cathie wondered if he'd ever do this for real. Take the chance? Put his heart on the line?

Before she could say a word, his head was coming down to hers, his arms closing around her. He touched his lips to hers and whispered, "I think we have an audience."

Cathie sank into the kiss and him. She felt his hesitation, felt his touch all the way down to her cold toes. Her nose was cold, too, and his face and his lips were warm. He took the barest taste of her mouth, holding her so softly, like she was a most expensive piece of something terribly fragile and extremely rare.

Just like this, she thought. *Touch me just like this.*

Dangerous thoughts for a woman whose marriage was supposed to be about anything but love.

Christmas made it easier to pretend and to get lost in the crowd. As Matt predicted, the house was spilling over with people.

Hours slipped away, the wedding rushing closer.

She got more nervous every minute, couldn't help but think, *What if I misread the signs?* What if there hadn't been signs at all? Just coincidences she'd assigned some meaning to, because she'd wanted so much to believe it was possible for her to have him, that it was meant to be?

What kind of mistake was she making?

She'd brought the Box with her, had hidden it in

the back of a drawer, and she kept pulling it out and staring at the thing.

Faith was an odd thing.

A hard thing.

Believing in things you couldn't see or hear or ever really completely understand.

Matt didn't believe in anything but himself and his own abilities and willingness to work hard to get what he wanted. He'd have said anything more than that was not only unnecessary but foolish.

If anyone needed a lesson in faith and love, it was him.

Which was likely her wanting to justify what she was doing, to somehow make it right.

Could I just have the big, booming voice? A quick, simple Marry Matt *would do nicely.*

Cathie frowned and heard nothing. Of course, she'd probably really lose it if the Box ever started talking back to her.

The day rushed on. Her cousins, aunts and mother surprised her with a wedding shower that night. The presents were beautiful, all lingerie, silk and lace, both pretty and sexy. She blushed and couldn't begin to imagine wearing them for Matt.

Would they ever have a night like that? Would he even want her that way?

Which made her think of something else, every bit as unsettling as whether or not he had a girlfriend. They'd left out one other important detail.

Sex.

Was he going to be celibate for the next three years? She hadn't asked him to honor their marriage vows in any way, didn't think she had the right. It was three years, after all. She couldn't imagine a man like Matt…not for three years.

"Cathie, you okay?" her mother asked.

She looked up to find all eyes on her. "Fine," she lied. "Where's Matt?"

"Your brothers dragged him off somewhere," her aunt Margaret said.

For some abbreviated version of a bachelor party, no doubt.

Her party broke up not long after that when she pleaded tiredness and wanting to get a good night's sleep. Her mother fussed over her for a moment and then let her go to her room.

The minute the door closed behind her, Cathie grabbed the phone and dialed Matt's cellphone. He answered on the second ring. She could hear laughter in the background—her brothers and cousins—and someone teasing, asking who was on the phone and if Cathie was already checking up on him. *Like a wife.*

"Hi," she said. "It's me."

"Hang on." Matt told the others he needed a moment, took some wild ribbing about that, and then it got quieter and he said, "What's wrong?"

"I need to talk to you, and I'm sorry for interrupting. I won't do that. I won't be like that. I promise."

"Cathie, just tell me what's wrong?" He sounded so patient, so understanding.

"We just…we forgot something else. Something I have to ask you. Not over the phone. It's important. I don't know if I can do this, Matt."

"Okay," he said. "Just hang on. Where are you?"

"In my bedroom. Mom gave me the tiny one at the end of the hall on the third floor." A luxury, because she wasn't sharing with anyone. The house was packed. "You know the one I mean."

"Sure. I'll be there. Just hang on. And don't say anything to anyone."

Fifteen minutes later, he slipped quietly into her room. She'd turned out the lights, because if anyone else came to find her, she wanted them to think she was asleep, and it was good, because this way, he wouldn't be able to see her so clearly.

She felt foolish and embarrassed. Panic was not far behind.

She sat, miserable and silent, in her bed, and Matt stood by her side, frowning down at her.

"Just one more day," he said. "You can do it, Cathie."

"I'm trying to, but…what about you? This is going to mess up your life."

"How?"

"Lots of ways."

He sat down on the bed, obviously thinking this was going to take a while. "Name one."

"What about your girlfriend?"

"What about her? I told you, it was nothing."

"What about sex?" *There.* She just said it, and she thought he'd grinned when she did.

"What about it?"

"What are you going to do? We never talked about it. It's three years, Matt, and I don't expect you to…to…you know?"

"Do without?" He did laugh then.

"Yes!" she said miserably. "And I guess it's really none of my business, anyway. I know that. And I'm sorry. Never mind. It's not even the most important thing.''

"And what is the most important thing?" he asked carefully.

"That I don't know if I can do this."

"Sure you can," he shot back.

"Marriage is supposed to mean something," she said. "I feel like I'm making a mockery of the whole thing. We have to stand in my father's church. He's going to ask us to repeat those vows, to make promises to each other—"

"So, you want to forget the whole thing?"

"I don't know!" she cried. "I don't know what to do."

"Well, I do, and I think you're just going to have to trust me on this. It's last-minute nerves. That's all. You have to think about your objective here. You want to keep your baby. You want to finish school and be able to support yourself. You don't want your family to freak out or your father to worry himself to death. There's only one way to accomplish that. By marrying me. Tomorrow."

"This isn't business, Matt. It's my life. Our lives."

"Same principle. You have a goal—to keep this baby—and you know what you have to do to meet your goal."

"The lies don't bother you? The vows?"

He sighed. "They're just words, Cathie. All we have to do is say the words. This agreement is between you and me, and no one else. And we both know exactly what that agreement is."

"But what if…what if we want something else? I mean, if things change, in time?"

"Whatever comes along, we'll deal with it," he said. "If you meet someone, you want out, all you have to do is say so."

"What if you meet someone?"

"That's not going to happen," he claimed.

"You don't know that."

"I don't want to marry anyone. I never will. I mean, I'm willing, for you and for this baby." His arm came around her. Her head fell to his shoulder. He placed a kiss on her forehead. "This is a one-time deal. It's just for you."

And she hoped she was the only one for him.

The love she'd felt for him so long ago welled up inside of her. She'd tried so hard to dismiss it and to say that she was too young, that it was an infatuation, all those things before.

But the truth was, he'd always been the one.

The only reason she'd ever really looked at any other man was because she'd been so sure she'd never have him. That thing with Tim...she'd been waiting so long for what she thought of as her real life to start. All those years she'd spent at home, helping take care of her father and keep the family business going, waiting for her chance to get away, be on her own, to find someone and fall in love.

She'd been so ready when Tim had shown up, had wanted to fall in love much more than she'd wanted to love him specifically.

What a fool she'd been.

And Matt was coming to her rescue. She buried her face in his neck, and thought about telling him everything she'd ever felt for him, everything she still wanted from him. He'd be horrified, would explain as gently as possible that he simply didn't have those things to offer her or any woman.

She believed there was a well of love inside of him. It might be buried so deep he didn't even know it was there, but she believed.

There, she'd found one, little bit of faith. In Matt and the love he so completely dismissed as even a possibility.

Either that, or she was playing God with both his life and hers. And her baby's. Thinking she knew what was best for all of them.

She didn't know which it was.

"I'm scared, Matt," she said.

"I know, but I'm here, and I'll take care of you. I promise."

Matt woke up with an armful of woman. Soft, womanly curves draped over his body, snuggled close.

"Mmm," he said, his mouth finding her forehead. He thought about reaching for her mouth or about giving her hair a little tug to bring her face up, so he could kiss her for real.

Then he woke up a bit more and wondered who she was, where he was, why there was light coming in through the window at that angle. Light didn't hit him full in the face in the morning when he was in his own bed.

Squinting against the glare, he realized in a split second that he was at Cathie's parents' house, with Cathie in his arms, and unless she backed out, this would be their wedding day.

He blinked, managing to bring everything into focus. It was morning. He was in her bed. And Cathie's mother was standing in the doorway frowning at him.

Oh, hell. He'd fallen asleep.

He glanced down, reassured that both he and Cathie were fully clothed, on top of the covers, where they'd fallen asleep the night before. Cathie hadn't yet woken up, and he didn't want her to. He held up one finger, signaling to Mary that he needed a minute, and she backed out of the room without a word.

Matt carefully slid his arm from beneath Cathie's head. She looked so vulnerable. It wasn't hard to still see something of the girl who'd meant so much to him, the one who'd believed in him when no one else did.

This was payback time of a different sort, he realized. Not about what he owed her family, but about what he owed *her.*

He smoothed down his shirt, tucked it in on the side where it had come untucked, brushed a hand through his hair, thinking of all the times to get caught in Cathie's bed....

He went into the hall and faced Cathie's mother, wondering how much he'd have to tell her. But before he could get out a word, Mary said, "Hold that thought. We might as well do this in Jim's study, so you don't have to go through the whole thing again with him."

"Fine." He followed her down the stairs and into the reverend's study, the scene of many discussions in Matt's life. About fighting at school, swearing, missing money that he actually hadn't taken, times the cops had picked him up just because they knew what he was like. All sorts of good things.

He never thought he'd be here trying to explain something like this.

"I found the missing groom," Mary said. "In your daughter's bed."

Jim Baldwin, his hair whiter than it used to be, with more lines in his face but still a steely-eyed stare when it suited him, sat behind his desk looking pointedly at Matt, waiting for an explanation.

Matt didn't know what to say. Jim wasn't a prude. He might make noises about frowning on the idea of anyone sleeping with his daughter before marrying her, but the man lived in the real word. He would not be shocked.

It might be that he saw this as a lack of respect, sneaking into Cathie's bed in the Baldwins' house. And it might even have something to do with all the traditions having to do with a wedding. Matt wasn't even sure about that.

"Looks like they fell asleep talking," Mary said, turning to Matt. "Which is fine. I'm just wondering how much you could possibly have to talk about at this late date. What would be so important that it couldn't wait until after the wedding? Unless this is about whether we've having a wedding?"

Leave it to Mary to cut right to it.

"Cathie was a little nervous last night," he admitted.

"She's more than a little nervous," Mary said. "And I've tried not to pry, but I think there's something going on here that the two of you aren't telling us, Matt."

"And you may think it's none of our business, son, as her parents. But I'm also the man who's going to marry the two of you, and I don't do that when I have doubts that the couple is sure they know what they're doing. Normally, I won't even perform a wedding without meeting with the couple several times in advance and satisfying myself that they seem ready to take on this kind of commitment. Too many people just rush into things like this. I may need to treat you and Cathie like any other couple today. Unless you can clear this up for me, fast, I won't marry you.''

Well, hell.

The morning just kept getting worse.

Matt looked from Jim to Mary, weighing his options.

''Don't even try that with me,'' Mary said.

''What?'' he asked.

''That bit where you try to figure out just how much of the truth you have to tell me to satisfy me.''

Jeez, the woman was good, even after all this time.

''All right.'' Matt shook his head and grinned and stuck with the truth. At least, with part of it, wondering if he could still pull one over on Mary when it counted. ''Cathie really didn't want the two of you to know this, because she's concerned about upsetting you and disappointing you. But the thing is…she just found out she's pregnant.''

It was a calculated risk. They weren't letting him go without getting something out of him, and if Jim got Cathie in here and started grilling her, she wouldn't last five minutes. Plus, they'd know about the baby soon anyway. If they assumed she just found out two or three days ago, instead of three weeks ago…. Well, they could just assume that.

He looked at Mary first, who seemed torn between

concern and out-and-out joy. He thought things were going to be okay. Mary had been talking about grandchildren since her oldest son graduated from college ten years ago. So far, she didn't have any. Jim did not look so pleased, but he wasn't losing it, either. But then, Jim Baldwin didn't lose it. He'd worry, but Matt didn't think the man knew how to yell. He was a model of patience, and he loved Cathie more than just about anyone on earth.

"I'm sorry. I should have been more careful with her," he said. Which was the truth. He should have beaten the hell out of her professor. Hell, he would when they got back to town.

"Yes, you should have," Jim said, trying for sternness.

"A baby?" Mary asked, pure awe in her voice.

Matt nodded.

Mary looked at her husband and said, "Our little girl's going to have a baby." Like she couldn't quite believe it.

"She's not even done with school," Jim said. "And she waited so long and worked so hard to get there."

"I'll see that she has a chance to finish, if that's what she wants," Matt promised. As long as nobody asked if he was the father, they were home-free, and Jim and Mary would never ask that. They'd never think Cathie would have fallen into bed with some jerk who'd left her pregnant and alone.

"She should finish," Mary said. "It's important that a woman have a way to support herself. But she'll want to be home with the baby, too. I know she will."

"We'll work it out," Matt said.

"Oh, dear lord. A baby," Mary said, and then

walked over to Matt and grabbed him, tears of joy on her face. "I knew something was wrong. I just knew it. But this…oh, this wonderful. I mean…this is what you want, Matt, isn't it?"

"Yes." He wanted to make this right for Cathie. "Cathie's always wanted children. We all know that. Other than worrying about the reaction from the two of you…."

Okay, that was a big, fat lie, and he actually felt guilty about telling it. But what was he supposed to do?

Mary was too in awe of the idea of being a grandmother to notice, and Jim looked like he was trying to be reverendly and fatherly, but the grandfather-to-be in him just wouldn't let him.

"I hear the first grandchild in the family always gets spoiled rotten," Matt said.

"And you will not deny me a moment of that pleasure," Mary insisted.

"No, I won't. But I'd really appreciate it if we could not let Cathie know that the two of you know. She'll tell you in time, I know, but today…she's been a little emotional since she found out, and feeling guilty about getting things out of order. I don't want her to have one more thing to worry about today."

"Oh, dear. I can see her doing exactly that, and I suppose now I'm going to have to worry about keeping a secret from her," Mary said. "If she's anything like me, she'll be on the verge of tears for the whole nine months."

"That bad?" Matt frowned.

"Yes, that bad," Jim said. "And we don't want the

bride in tears before the wedding, if we can help it. All right. We'll keep this between the three of us."

"Okay. I can do it." Mary took a breath, fortifying herself. "A baby!"

"Darling," Jim suggested, "why don't you go try to pull yourself together and give me and Matt a chance to talk."

Mary, who was facing Matt at the moment, grinned and mouthed the words *Don't worry, it'll be fine,* before she hugged him one more time. "I want a lot of grandchildren. A whole house full. Say, 'Yes, Mom.'"

"Yes, Mom," he repeated dutifully. He'd never called her Mom, although she'd invited him to on more than one occasion.

Mary left, and he turned to Jim, waiting for a grilling that never came.

All Jim said was, "You promised me you'd take good care of her."

"I will."

"And if you ever hurt her…"

"I understand."

"I'm going to talk to her about this. Not about the baby, but I will ask about this marriage. I have to know this is what she wants—"

"It is," Matt said.

"Then there won't be any harm in asking," Jim said, and then he shook his head in wonder. "A baby?"

Matt nodded. What was it about babies? He just didn't get it. As he saw it, they were a lot like puppies. They made a lot of noise and a lot of messes. Communicating with them was difficult, at best. People held them and fed them and fussed over them, and generally went crazy over them. What was the big deal? Cathie would be just that way. He'd have expected it from her and Mary. But Jim?

"It doesn't seem like that long ago that we brought Cathie home from the hospital," he said wistfully. "She was a surprise, too. A big one. Four little boys are enough to drive a good woman mad, especially when she had a husband who's gone so much, and Mary blamed me. Not just for being gone, but for the four boys and for getting her pregnant with Cathie. We weren't exactly prepared for another one, and it took some…adjusting."

"I'm sure." *Five kids?*

"I hadn't thought about that in years—how rocky things were when we found out," Jim said. "But, I tell you, from the moment I held that little girl in my arms for the first time…she is one of the great joys of my life."

"I know." And this man was about to entrust one of his greatest treasure to Matt, who was going to accept, feeling like the worst kind of impostor. She deserved so much better.

"I remember the way she looked at you when we first brought you here, like we weren't bringing you into the family. We were bringing you to her and her alone. She was so sure you belonged with us."

Matt remembered thinking they were all nuts, not just to trust him with their material things, but something as precious as their daughter? Not that he ever would have hurt her. But there were lots of bad-assed kids on the streets who would have.

She'd latched onto him in a way he still didn't understand, with a kind of faith and constancy that had been completely missing in his life to that point, and if he had to look back over his life and think about joy, she was it. Frustrating and funny and way too trusting for her own good, and a complete joy, at a time when he'd been doing his best to show nothing but his tough-guy side to the world.

He probably owed her even more than he owed her parents.

"Jim, I would do anything for her." It was one of the truest things he'd ever said in his life. "I would give her anything in this world that's within my power to give."

Cathie's father nodded, looking satisfied. "That's what I was waiting to hear, son. That's the only way I'd give her to you, if I believed you felt that way about her."

Chapter Five

Once he escaped from Jim's study, no one let Matt near Cathie. She was being guarded by a half-dozen women, who started chattering like riled-up birds whenever he got close to the room where she was closeted with her mother and a favorite cousin of hers.

Her brothers were all giving him hell about skipping out of the bachelor party, claiming he was henpecked already, then riding him about where he'd been all night. Teasing publicly, but each and every one of them had taken him aside and given him a stern warning that he'd better have been with his bride-to-be, soothing a case of last-minute jitters. Or else.

All he wanted now was to talk to her, to make sure she was okay.

That she'd still be walking down the aisle to him later that day.

There were all sorts of emotions rumbling around inside of him, set off by her father's words, images of Cathie as a girl, times when she'd been so stubborn, so determined to draw him into her world. Times when she'd pestered him mercilessly. When she'd been his champion to the whole, wide world, so sure he was so much smarter and so much better a person than he ever imagined he'd be.

All of it ruined by her deciding she was in love with him at sixteen.

She couldn't be in love with him now. She was carrying another man's child, and he knew her. She wouldn't have climbed into bed with a man unless she believed she was in love with him, and she wasn't the kind of person to think she could love two men at the same time.

So she must have gotten over Matt long ago and fallen in love with this jerk. She was just in trouble, and Matt was trying to help her.

That was it.

Nothing to do with love at all.

Hell, she might still be hung up on that scum who'd gotten her pregnant.

And all that was happening today was nothing more than a charade to appease her family.

"You look a little nervous, son." Jim clapped a hand on Matt's back as they stood in his office in the church, watching the clock roll down the last ten minutes before the ceremony was scheduled to begin.

"I just want it done," Matt said.

Jim laughed. "I felt the same way myself when I married Mary."

"Cathie's okay?"

Jim nodded. "Mary managed not to say anything and mostly not to cry. So you just hang on. Another thirty minutes or so, and the nerve-racking part will be over. Then you can get started on the fun part of being married, and then the really hard part of staying married."

Matt just glared at him.

Jim laughed again. "I was worried about you. You didn't look nervous at all until this morning in my study. It looked like you didn't have any idea what you were getting into."

"I'm glad you're enjoying this, Jim."

"Could we make it Dad? Finally?"

Matt had never called him that, despite repeated invitations.

"There's always been a place for you here, Matt. All you had to do was accept it. You marry my daughter, you automatically have a place in this family."

"So that means this time, if you need something from me, I'm family, and you're going to take it," Matt said.

"You're still upset about that?"

"You'd been telling me I was family for years, and the first time I try to act like it, you turned me down." He'd offered them money, a lot of it, when Jim had been in the hospital waiting for a heart transplant.

"And you thought I was rejecting you and not the money, didn't you?" Jim shook his head. "Sorry. I didn't think of it that way. Not until later, after I'd already turned you down."

"I wanted to do it," Matt said. "You needed it. I

had it. It was one of the first things I'd actually wanted to do with all that money I made.''

''And I should have let you. I think my pride was taking a beating, and I let it get the best of me. It was the first time in my life I was worried about being able to support my family. I wasn't handling it well. You know something about pride, don't you, son?''

''Maybe,'' he admitted. ''Cathie's still worried. Not about the money part, but about your health. Is everything okay?''

Jim shrugged it off. ''Things happen from time to time. Little blips here and there. They watch me pretty closely, run all sorts of tests, and Mary frets every time it happens. We try to spare the kids as much of that as we can. But my new heart's fine right now, and I'm hoping to keep it that way. Especially now that I'm going to be a grandfather.''

''There's nothing you need?''

''Not right now.'' Jim hesitated. ''I worry about what would happen to Mary, if anything happened to me. We got through the transplant, but it took just about everything we had set aside for our retirement. Not that I plan to ever retire. I love what I'm doing. Mary does, too. But still, if something happened to me, I worry about how she'd make it.''

''You don't have to worry about that,'' Matt said quietly. ''At least, as long as she's not as stubborn as you, when it comes to letting someone help her.''

''Thank you, Matt. You're a good man. You tell Mary, if the time ever comes, that we talked about you helping out that way. That it's what I wanted her to do.''

"Oh, she'll love that. You won't take anything from me, but you expect her to?"

"She would have a thing or two to say about that. I guess I'll just have to stick around and take care of her myself. Now, are you ready to get married?"

"As ready as I'll ever be."

Matt took his place at the front of the little church, Cathie's father on one side of him and her brother, Jack, on the other. Her oldest brother, Brett, had the honor of walking her down the aisle, and the other two, not willing to be left out of the ceremony, had taken the only spots left—those of bridesmaids.

"Can't wait to see them fighting over the bouquet," Jim said, as the two walked down the aisle in matching tuxedos.

Matt stood there and told himself to breathe. He'd taken part in solving corporate espionage cases that had been easier than this, and why, he couldn't understand.

It was nothing. He'd told himself and her that often enough.

And then Cathie appeared in the doorway at the back of the church, and he couldn't see anything but her, as beautiful and grown up as he'd ever imagined her being.

The dress was deceptively simple, a heavy white satin faded to cream, no lace at all. It caressed her breasts, held up at her shoulders by tiny bows, gathered tightly at her waist and then spread out into a billowing skirt that hung to her feet.

Simple as could be.

Her hair was piled up on her head, little curls dangling down here and there, diamond studs he'd left with Mary to give to her this morning as a wedding gift twinkling in her ears.

"Takes your breath away, doesn't she?" her father whispered.

Her brother glanced over at Matt and laughed softly. Matt thought he might have swayed on his feet, which was ridiculous, but still, that's what he thought happened.

Music filled the church, and Cathie walked slowly toward him.

He couldn't take his eyes off of her. Any hope he'd ever had of thinking of her as a little girl was gone forever. The girl had clearly grown up.

She looked heartbreakingly tentative as she let go of her brother's arm and slipped her hand through the crook of Matt's. Her hand rested on his arm, and he put his other hand on top of hers, to hold her there, in case she had any ideas of running away.

Vaguely, thoughts of what she'd said last night— about his sex life or lack thereof once they were married—flitted through his head.

He hadn't thought it would be a problem. He traveled a lot. He could take care of things that way. It wasn't the ideal situation, but that way, it would never touch her, never hurt her. It would just be a way of getting through, and that's all they had to do—get through the time he'd promised her, the time he owed her.

It seemed sordid now and completely unsatisfactory to ever think of treating her that way.

Three years? What was he supposed to do for three years?

She looked up at him questioningly, what might have been panic flitting through her eyes. He leaned down until his lips brushed the rim of her ear and said, "You are so beautiful."

She gave him a weak smile and mouthed, "Thank you. Don't let go."

"I won't."

The ceremony was mostly a blur. He was aware of her by his side and the light of the candles, rays of sunlight streaming through the stained glass, of speaking those vows that had so troubled her, and Cathie's own trembling responses.

And then Jim said Matt could kiss his bride.

He took a breath, bracing himself, and then took her gently in his arms, like she was the most beautiful and fragile thing on earth and he was worried about breaking her, which he was.

He settled her against him, and then took her face in one of his hands and tilted her head up to his. Her lips were soft and tentative beneath his, and a kind of hunger he'd have thought he'd trampled out long ago, leaped up inside of him at the first touch.

He pulled back, gentling the kiss when every instinct in him said to go deeper, to take everything he could from her with just a kiss. It wasn't going to be that way. This wasn't about him. It was about her and what she needed, what he'd agreed to provide.

But he could touch her every now and then, and it wasn't often he'd have a formal invitation to do so. So he made the most of the moment, working his way slowly and completely along her soft, sweet lips, until she clung to him, and he forget everything about where they were and what they were supposed to be doing. Everything but the taste of her and the fresh, clean smell of her skin and the softness of her body pressed to his.

Laughter erupted from somewhere in the back of the church, building as it moved through the congregation. Someone whooped and cheered, and Cathie's father laughed.

Matt finally came up for air, seeing the stunned look on her face for just an instant before one of her brothers swung her into his arms and kissed her. They lined up and passed her down the line, from one of their arms to another, while she cried and smiled and kissed them all.

Matt watched her go. People were slapping him on the back and laughing and all talking at once, and he was still trying to figure out exactly what had happened.

He couldn't want her like that.

It wasn't any part of their agreement.

"Don't worry," Cathie's father told him. "They'll bring her back."

"What?" Matt said.

"You looked like you were about to go grab her and haul her back over here to you." Jim laughed again, slapping him on the back. "Just try to be patient for another hour or two, okay, and then you can take her away. If you're very, very fortunate, you'll still be looking at her that way fifty years from now and thinking she's just as beautiful to you then as she is today."

"Jim—"

"I'm happy for you, Matt. Happy for you both. I can't wait to see this baby."

Yes, *the baby.*

The reason they were doing this whole thing.

He had to remember that, had to keep his head and try to find a way not to let himself get too close to his wife.

In every fantasy wedding Cathie had ever imagined, when she looked down the aisle of the church, the man standing at the end of it was always Matt.

If she hadn't been so nervous, it would have been easy to pretend this was just another one of those fantasies. She'd marry Matt, right here in her father's little church in the mountains with her whole family looking on, and someday she'd have Matt's babies, and he would love her.

But she was nervous and sad and hopeful and feeling guilty about being pregnant with another man's child, about standing here in her grandmother's dress with all the faces of the people she loved beaming back at her as she stood at the back of the church, ready to make her way down the aisle.

Matt was there, and he had the oddest look on his face. It was like he was willing her to come to him. Somehow, she found the courage to just keep walking. No matter how hard she'd tried, she'd never been able to get that far away from him. He held her heart with invisible strings, ones she'd never been able to sever, and there were moments when she thought she held his, battered and bruised as it was.

She wondered if it was possible to will a man to love her, to draw him into her so completely that he could never get away, never run. So that there was nothing to do but stay and face his feelings honestly and openly. To find a way to trust her and to trust in love.

She made it to Matt's side and let everything else become a blur. He took her hand, told her she was beautiful and sounded like he meant it, something flaring in his eyes. The vows were a jumble of words, the images oddly hazy, as were the sensations.

Until he kissed her.

Really kissed her.

She clung to him, melted into him. He looked as dazed as she felt when they finally came up for air. Vaguely, she heard the laughter and the teasing, felt tears rolling down her cheeks, and then someone drew her away to congratulate her.

It seemed to go on forever, all the people so happy and ready to celebrate. Cathie went with the flow, smiling until her face hurt and trying not to cry. The day was such a jumble of emotions, no one thought a thing of it. Her mother cried. Her aunts cried. Her brothers and her father nearly cried, and she was trying hard not to even look at her groom, so handsome in his tuxedo, not a hair out of place, looking like a curious mix of her bad boy and a sexy stranger.

What in the world was she going to do with him now?

All too soon, Cathie found herself hustled upstairs to get dressed, so she and Matt could catch their plane. She barely managed not to say, ''What plane?'' Was it a story he'd concocted to get them out of here or were they really going somewhere?

She felt dizzy, like she'd really had champagne, instead of pretended to sip it.

Upstairs in her tiny bedroom, she stood staring at

the bed. She'd woken this morning alone, with nothing but the memory of the feel of his arms around her, and the memory had helped her make it through the day.

Now she was supposed to actually live with Matt.

How was that going to work?

Was she going to try to win his heart? Did she have the courage?

Cathie quickly packed the last of her things in her carry-on bag. Makeup, toiletries, the satin and lace shower presents. What else?

She couldn't think of anything. Nothing left to do but get out of her gown and get dressed. Cathie undid the ties at her shoulders and pressed an arm against her breasts to keep the bodice from falling down. The gown flared at the bustline, but fit tight along her rib cage, held there by tiny buttons up and down the left side of the dress, under her arm. She hadn't even tried to button them herself when she'd gotten into the dress. Her hands had been shaking, and her mother had taken over the task.

She twisted around as best she could, trying to get a good grip with her left hand, then her right, and that's when she spotted the Box on the floor beneath her bed. She'd almost forgotten it.

She'd stashed it there earlier, when her aunt Margaret had almost caught Cathie talking to it before the wedding, looking for some last-minute reassurance. She really had to stop talking to that thing. Cathie nudged it out from under the bed with her foot and picked it up. Looking down into her carry-on, she saw it was going to land amidst a pile of lingerie.

The good girl in her winced.

Sorry. She tucked it into the bag, right there against a hot-pink teddy that made most of her swimwear look modest. What had her cousin Jane been thinking? *That Matt was one of the sexiest men on earth.* At least, that's what Jane had said. Cathie pulled the Box out of the pink fluffy thing, simply unable to stand having it there, and wrapped it up in virginal white satin instead. *Better?* Yes, that was better.

She was a very good girl, after all. Always had been, at least.

And now she got to live with Matt?

A sudden attack of nerves had her looking down into her carry-on and whispering, *If you've got any ideas...*

Right on cue, there was a knock on the door.

Cathie whirled around staring from the door to the Box, afraid to say anything else to it. This was so weird. She called out, ''Come in,'' expecting her mother or her cousin, finding Matt instead. He'd ditched the tuxedo in favor of a severe black suit that had obviously been made just for him.

He looked polished and expensive, like a man who was used to getting exactly what he wanted in life, which she knew wasn't true at all. At least, not until about seven years ago, when the world had turned his way. At least in terms of money, success, power and respect.

But not love.

Did he even want it? If she offered it to him, freely and fully, what would he do? Most likely, explain to her the fallacy of even believing in it.

''Hi,'' he said softly, still standing by the door.

''Hi.'' She felt more awkward than she had the first

time she'd seen him after she'd thrown herself at him at sixteen.

"It's getting late. We need to hurry."

"Oh. Okay." She pressed the bodice of the dress more tightly against her. "I just need to get out of this. It won't take a minute."

Matt frowned. "Do you need help?"

"Well…yes. If you don't mind." The dress was heavy satin and fully lined. She hadn't worn a bra, which meant there was nothing between her bare skin and him except her own arms and a bit of satin.

Cathie felt his gaze on her skin. Suddenly, she was warm and tingly all over, like he'd really touched her, not just looked at her.

Did he really think she was beautiful?

Would that help? After all, he'd been surrounded by gorgeous women for years, and none of them had won his heart. She didn't think anyone had even come close.

Still, if it was all she had to work with…

Cathie tried to think logically. Sex was a perfectly normal part of marriage, and she was married. She loved her husband.

But he didn't love her.

But maybe he would one day.

But the marriage wasn't supposed to be real. They'd made a deal.

But he wasn't happy the way he was. How could he be? And he'd probably never let another woman as close to him as she could get in the three years they were supposed to be together. He needed her, needed all the love she could give him.

There, she'd almost managed to make seducing him

sound noble. Her, a woman who had a God Box wrapped up in a negligee in the suitcase on her bed.

Good girls just weren't cut out for seduction. Were they?

"It buttons here." Cathie turned so her side was facing him and lifted one arm out of the way, so he could see all those tiny buttons. "I can't get my hand twisted the right way."

Matt frowned down at her and didn't move a muscle at first, something she found immensely encouraging.

There had been a time when she could have sworn he was attracted to her, which had led her to throw herself at him one night when he was home from college. He hadn't been able to get away from her fast enough. They really didn't have to play that scene again, did they?

Assuming it would end the same way?

Matt sat down on the bed, which put him at eye-level with all her buttons, and right beside her carry-on. Cathie closed her eyes, held onto her dress and tried not to think about anything. The buttons were tiny. His hands were big and warm.

He swore as he struggled with a particularly stubborn one. "How do women get in and out of these things?"

"With help." The dress gaped open. Cool air rushed over her heated skin, and she shivered.

"Almost done," he said.

For one, wild, reckless moment, Cathie thought about letting the dress drop to her waist and throwing herself into his arms. Honestly, it seemed she had no shame.

Well...obviously, she did, because she didn't actually do it. She suspected most of the women he knew would have.

"Done." Matt stood up. She didn't think his breath was quite steady, but didn't have the nerve to look at him and make sure. But she could feel his gaze on her. It was like there were a million unanswered questions swirling around in the room, and neither one of them dared get near a one.

Cathie thought about simply telling him she wanted to make him happy, really happy for the first time in his life. Which had her thinking of what she truly had to offer him. She believed in him, believed he could do anything, always had. But that wasn't in question anymore. He was an amazing success. She'd tried making him a part of her family, but he'd always rejected that. She'd tried teasing him, tried making him laugh, but had seldom gotten very far with that. She could be kind and supportive. She doubted many people had been either of those things to him. But a man like him didn't come to love a woman for her kindness or support.

She was going to have to shake him out of his comfort zone, get behind those walls of his, if she had a chance of winning his heart. How did she do that?

"Anything else you need?" he asked warily.

"No." Cathie hugged her dress more tightly to her, feeling ridiculously vulnerable and inadequate to show this man anything about love.

"Good. Like I said, we need to hurry."

"Matt, wait." She closed her eyes. "Where do we go from here?"

"The Caribbean," he said, surely being deliberately

obtuse. He was a man, after all. "We have a reservation on a five o'clock flight out of Asheville."

"Oh." A honeymoon with Matt? "We don't have to do that."

"Cathie, I was going anyway. I couldn't very well go without you. Especially not the day we got married."

"I know, but...it's expensive, and—"

"We promised not to argue about money, remember?"

"I remember." It was one of the few things he'd asked of her, and it was proving hard. "I thought we were talking about money for necessities."

"I consider it a necessity," he claimed. Right along with the beautiful engagement ring he'd had made for her and the big, sparkly diamond earrings? "Besides, I want you to see the island. The water's unbelievably blue and so clear. The first time I saw the place, I thought about you."

"Oh." He'd reduced her speech capacity to a single syllable. *He'd thought of her there?* Well, okay. They could go. She wouldn't even grumble about the expense.

Cathie finally looked up at him and might have caught him looking down her dress. She couldn't be absolutely sure. A soft heat flared between them. She took a breath, and it was only in the midst of it that she felt her breasts rise against the bodice she clutched against her. He sucked in a breath of his own, and she wished she had the courage to just throw herself into his arms once again. Maybe it wouldn't be so bad to repeat that scene. Maybe it would end differently this time. She wasn't sixteen anymore, and she was his wife.

"Anything else you need?" he asked warily.

"No." But suddenly, three years seemed like a desperately short amount of time. "Wait. Yes. There is. Just one thing."

As she saw it, there weren't a lot of options here. She didn't think she could pull off a seduction of any kind. Not her. Brutal honesty? That wasn't all that appealing, either. Directness? She could do direct, couldn't she?

"We never settled anything before," she said. "When we were talking about how we were going to handle things, now that we're married. About you and…sex. What are you going to do, Matt?"

He backed up and frowned at her, as if he couldn't quite believe she'd said it. She couldn't, either. How was that for direct?

"I'm not going to do anything tonight. That's for sure," he said. "It's been a long day. It'll have been an even longer one by the time we're settled on the island."

"I wasn't talking about tonight. I was thinking about three years—"

"Cathie, we don't have to figure this out now."

"I know. I just…I can't tell you what to do. I don't feel like I have the right. But, just so you know, when you're trying to figure it out…" She closed her eyes and rushed on, forcing out the words. "We could…well, you could be with me."

Dead silence greeted her words.

Finally, her desire to know what he thought about her offer overcame her embarrassment. She opened her eyes. He stood before her like a man who might have been carved in stone, one who wasn't moving a single muscle in his entire body.

"If you wanted to," she added. Then thought of one more thing. "Just me. For the time we're together."

"What is this?" He swore softly into the darkness, turning his head away, then faced her again, something that looked near to fury on his face. "Some new form of thanking me? No more, Cathie. I'm the one paying back a debt here. You don't owe me anything."

"I know. I didn't mean it like that. I just thought...it made sense." It did to her. She was in love with him. She wanted to be with him. "If you wanted to be with me."

"If I wanted to?" he repeated.

Her face positively burned. She managed to nod somehow. "It just seems...easier."

"It would not be easy," he argued.

She wasn't at all sure what he meant. He was a man. She was a woman and his wife. How difficult could it be? "Look, if you don't want to—"

He swore once more, then sucked in air, his shoulders rising and falling slowly and deliberately with the effort. When he turned to face her, he said, "Are you trying to make me crazy?"

"No," she whispered. "I'm trying to make things...easier."

But he'd said, *It would not be easy.*

So, what would it be?

She risked a glance at his face, got scared at the harsh expression there and let her gaze drift downward. He'd always had a sleek, powerful build, but over the years he'd filled out beautifully. Wide shoulders, muscles she could feel in his upper arms, a hard, flat stomach, nice, slim hips and thighs.

He was dark and dangerous-looking and beautiful.

Her experiences with that other man...it had been fine. Better than fine. It had been...well, it was hard to say exactly. She'd waited so long, had so many dreams about it, years of restless longing. Understanding the mechanics of it couldn't come close to the experience of the real thing.

It had all been so new and good, and she'd tried to convince herself it had been more, that she'd been in love and that it hadn't been awkward or a little bit sad. That she was growing up, and this was what grown women did, and they liked it. She'd liked it. But, standing here with Matt, she couldn't help but think there was so much more she'd feel with him.

Cathie worked up her courage and took a step closer to him. She could swear he was fighting the urge to back away, that it was only force of habit—he never backed away from anything—that kept him where he was.

"I'm just trying to be reasonable about this," she claimed. It wasn't exactly a lie. "I mean, we'll be living together in the same house for three years. It just seems natural that at some point along the way, we'd...be together. Doesn't it?"

"Really? How many guys have you lived with, Cathie?"

"None." He would be the first for that. She was starting to regret ever starting this conversation. "Look, it's no big deal—"

"Oh, it's a big deal all right."

Now, that was definitely sexual innuendo. She couldn't help but take the briefest of glances down at his waist, and then below…. "Oh."

He made a choking sound, and he was furious. He grabbed her by the arms and her dress began to slip down, and the only way he could catch it quickly enough was to pull her hard against him.

"Oh," she said again, feeling…everything.

He was still choking. She was struggling not to let sheer elation show.

His hands went to her back, catching the dress and pulling it up, then sliding around to the sides, tugging it up some more. At least, she was sure that's what he meant to do. But on her left side, where the buttons had been, there was nothing but bare skin. Very sensitive, bare skin.

His hand landed there, at the side of her breast. He sucked in a breath. His hand hovered, not quite touching her, and she couldn't have that. She leaned into him, put the soft weight of the side of her breast into his hand.

His jaw went tight, his body rigid. Everywhere. Against her belly, he was hard and throbbing.

"Would it be so bad?" she asked, letting her entire body sink into his. Honestly, it was like her body had a mind of its own and had turned positively shameless.

"Yes," he said. "Give me a minute and I'll remember why."

But she couldn't afford to give him time to think. She gave up on salvaging her pride, on her natural reticence when it came to men and even her concern about holding up her dress. She wrapped her arms around his neck and pulled his head down to hers, his mouth meeting hers eagerly. His hand slid inside her open dress to her back, gliding across her skin, down to cup one of her hips in his palm and settle her closer against his lower body. The throbbing intensified.

She held his face in her hands, felt the slight roughness to his jaw and thought about how much she liked the feel of his skin on hers, his mouth, his hands.

His thumb teased at the tender side of her breast, stroking it, taking in more and more of it, until she ached to have his whole hand on her. Just his hand. Surely she could have that. Her body felt aching and empty and on fire in a way it had never been before, and he was her husband. He backed her up against the wall and devoured her with his mouth, while she clung to him and tried to get closer, to get completely inside him.

Finally, finally, his thumb rubbed across her nipple, and he buried his face in the side of her neck. She gasped and shivered, joy shimmering through her entire body.

She was going to be his.

His mouth came back to hers. She smiled as his lips closed around hers. Couldn't help herself. It was Matt.

And then from what seemed like a million miles away, someone called her name. She frowned, not even sure what planet she was on at the moment. Matt swore softly and pulled away.

"Cathie, it's almost three, and Matt said you two had to hurry or—"

Her mother stopped abruptly, two steps inside the room. Matt was standing between them, his body blocking as much as he could of Cathie's. She peered around his shoulder and gaped at her mother, while Matt, as discreetly as possible, pulled up her dress.

"I'm so sorry." Her mother grinned, not exactly looking sorry. "I thought…well, never mind. It's almost three."

Her mother backed out as fast as she could.

Cathie caught her breath and reminded herself she was over twenty-one and married. Getting caught in her bedroom in her parents' home with her dress down and with a member of the opposite sex was not really a problem.

Then she looked up into Matt's face.

Okay, it was a problem, because now that they'd been interrupted, he had time to think, and he obviously didn't like what he was thinking.

"Hold this," he said, putting the bodice of her dress into her hands.

"Okay."

He glared at her. "What the hell was that?"

Her trying to seduce him? No way she was going to admit that. Was this a trick question?

"It's all right," she said. "We're married."

He threw a look of sheer disgust. "Cathie, you know exactly what we are. This was not supposed to be a part of it."

"No, but why couldn't it be?"

It was like she'd told him the Earth was flat. What was so wrong with this idea? She could pick up with her *It would be so much simpler* argument, but that one hadn't gone over well the first time.

What would a woman of the world say now?

"Matt, if we both want it, why shouldn't we be together?"

He glared at her. "How long has that been your philosophy about sex?"

"Well—"

"I can answer that. *Never.*"

Okay, so he was right about that.

"You went to that jerk who got you pregnant a virgin, didn't you?"

Her first idea was to shoot back with something along the lines of *What if I did?* But that sounded particularly childish. "What does this have to do with anything?"

"It has to do with you and sex. This thing we're not supposed to have."

"Why not?"

"Because I know you. You don't do this just for the hell of it. Hell, you've hardly done it at all." He was practically shouting he was so mad.

"And why is that such a problem for you?"

"Because it's who you are, Cathie. What happened to you? How did you end up in this kind of a mess? Because you are the last person in the world I would have ever expected to find pregnant with some jerk of a guy's baby, especially a guy who's married and fooling around with one of his students."

"Well…" Cathie backed up against the wall, clutching her dress to her, tears filling her eyes, unable to believe how things had been going so well one minute and so completely wrong the next. Her bottom lip started to tremble. "That's what I did."

"Oh, hell, I'm sorry, Cathie. I didn't mean it like that."

"No, it's true. It's what happened."

"Don't cry," he said, coming reluctantly toward her again. "Please don't cry."

"I won't," she said, turning away to avoid his touch.

"I'm really sorry."

"It's not your fault." This was definitely hers. "Why don't you go ahead? I'll be right down."

"Okay." He left without another word.

She stepped carefully out of the dress, hugged it to her while she leaned against the wall and imagined a dozen different turns she might have taken in her life that would have changed everything. And wondering exactly why she'd ended up here, pregnant with another man's child and kind of married to Matt.

Chapter Six

They hardly said a word on the first, quick, commuter flight out of Asheville, then changed planes in Atlanta for a direct flight to San Juan.

Cathie sat silently in the first-class seats Matt had reserved, while the pretty, blond stewardess fussed over him, as she supposed most women did. She wondered if he'd ever thought about sharing his life with a woman? He seemed so terribly alone, always had. Success hadn't changed that in any way, and she didn't want him to be all alone, even if he didn't end up with her.

The plane made its final turn onto the long straightaway. The engines wound up for takeoff. It was fast and smooth. She was conscious of every inch of her husband's body next to hers. Despite the extra space of first class, he simply seemed to take up all the

room, sitting there so seemingly relaxed in these sur-
roundings.

The plane leveled off. The flight attendant came by
asking if there was anything she could get them. Matt
had a Scotch and soda. Cathie asked for a pillow. She
tucked it in between her head and the side of the plane,
shifting this way and that trying to get comfortable
without much success.

Matt downed the last of his Scotch, handed it to the
flight attendant, and then pushed the armrest between
them up and out of the way and said, "Come here."

She sat up, hesitated. He put his arm around her
shoulder and pulled her to him. "I'm sorry about what
I said earlier, in your room. I didn't mean it like that."

"I know." She let her head fall to his shoulder, but
kept her hands tucked against her chest. She didn't let
herself snuggle or anything, despite how good he
smelled and how comforting his hold was. Even if he
really didn't want her here. "You're going to think
I'm a lot more trouble than I'm worth."

"You've always been all kinds of trouble," he said
dryly. "Go to sleep, Cathie. It's been a long day, and
we've got hours to go."

She meant to just close her eyes and pretend to
sleep, because there was no telling when she'd manage
to get this close to him again, and it was so nice. But
the stress of the day had worn her out, and before she
knew it, she was asleep, waking only as the plane
touched down, finding herself wrapped all over Matt.

Oh, my.

It was like she didn't have a bone left in her body,
and he was her bed. She was completely relaxed and

enveloped in warmth, her nose buried in his suit, which smelled faintly of him.

She didn't ever want to move.

"Come on, sleepyhead," he said. "We're here."

She straightened slowly, feeling rumpled and relaxed as she hadn't in the longest time. He shifted in his seat, rolling his shoulder to loosen it up.

"Sorry," she said.

He gave her a look that seemed more than anything to say, *What in the world are we going to do?*

Good question.

She didn't even try to answer it, just smoothed her hair back into place and checked to make sure her clothes weren't too much of a mess.

From San Juan, they boarded a water taxi, which took them to a very private resort on its own island, a luxury Cathie had never even imagined.

"Just wait," Matt said, looking happy for the first time since she'd jumped him in the bedroom at her parents' home. "It's well worth the trip."

It was nearly one o'clock in the morning before the driver of what looked like a glorified golf cart dropped them off at the door of a tiny bungalow on the beach in the middle of nowhere. At least, it seemed that way at first, the foliage was so thick.

Cathie could hear the waves and the wind and wanted to see the ocean.

"It's just behind the bungalow," Matt said, his hand at the small of her back, steering her inside, once the driver had unlocked the door and handed Matt the keys. He gave the man a tip and said, "Just leave the suitcases inside the door. We'll handle it from here."

He steered Cathie through a small living room and

out the sliding glass door, which opened onto a small patio. She saw a hot tub in the corner, a table and chairs, a pair of chaise lounge chairs, a hammock off in the trees to the right and through the darkness, she could make out the whitecaps of the waves.

It seemed like they had a beach all to themselves.

This had definite possibilities.

"Kick your shoes off," Matt said. "You can dip your toes in the water."

He held her hand to help her keep her balance while she slipped off her shoes, then took off his own and his socks, rolled up his pant legs. Then he took her hand and led her onto the beach.

It opened up before them, a long, smooth line going as far as the eye could see in either direction. The sand was like powder beneath her feet, and there were faint lights here and there along the shoreline, but that was it.

"The hotel's just back there," Matt said, pointing to the left. "It's not very big. Most of the beach is lined with little bungalows like ours."

Cathie felt the breeze on her face, heard the swish of the waves. It was almost as if they were the only ones here at all. "It's beautiful, Matt."

"Wait until you see it in daylight."

They walked along the edge of the water a bit and didn't say any more. Matt finally led her back to the bungalow, and she said, "Thank you for bringing me here."

"Just try to enjoy it, Cathie. Rest and relax. You've done nothing but work and take care of other people and go to school for years. I want you to have a break. You've earned it."

"Thank you."

He hesitated. "I guess we should turn in. We have two bedrooms. Want the one on the left or the right?"

"I'll go left," she said.

He carried her suitcase into the room, which was a cool, classical white. There was a dainty white rug trimmed in delicate flowers. White rattan furniture. Gauzy white curtains and a mosquito netting draped over the bed and gathered at the four corners, obviously for decoration. A pristine, puffy, white comforter on the bed.

She sat down on the bed. Sank into it, was more like it. The mattress was soft and welcoming. She thought for just a moment about pulling Matt down with her and the way she'd sink even further into the mattress with him on top of her.

One more time, she felt the moments slipping away, like the three years allotted to her would never be enough.

He stood by the door, eager to get away, it seemed. "Go ahead and sleep in, in the morning, okay? We've got ten days, plenty of time."

"Okay."

"Good night."

"'Night," she said, trying not to think about being all alone on her wedding night.

Cathie took her overnight case into the sparkling white bathroom and quickly got ready for bed, thinking the busier she stayed, the less time she'd have to think about anything. Time for a nightgown. She had six, all shower gifts, ranging from skimpy to pretty and elegant. What she wanted was her soft, nearly threadbare, oversized T-shirt she normally slept in.

But a woman never knew what opportunities might come her way in the night. The most modest gown she had was a shimmering, ivory-colored silk with spaghetti straps and lots of pretty lace detailing the neckline that dipped low in back and in front, the one she'd wrapped the Box in.

She unwrapped it and shook out the gown, holding it in front of her, trying to gauge just how much skin would show, once she had it on.

"Not bad," she told her reflection in the bathroom mirror, then slipped the gown on.

In her bedroom, she unpacked quickly, finally ending up with nothing but the Box in her hand. Cathie went to put it in the drawer in the nightstand, but that was awfully close to the bed. Not that she was expecting any luck there. But still...

She opened her underwear drawer, but there was all that lingerie again. *No.*

There was the closet. It was as far from the bed as could be. Cathie took her carry-on bag, put the Box in there all by itself, zipped the bag and reached up on her tiptoes to put it on the top shelf, in the farthest corner of the closet, turned out the closet light and closed the doors. *There.* Just in case.

She was losing it, for sure, would not ask that thing for anything else. Wouldn't even think of it. No more lingerie anywhere near it. She clicked off the lights, drew back the covers of the bed and was just about to climb in when she heard a faint tapping on her bedroom door.

"Cathie? I think I need to—"

She opened the door and found Matt standing there in shorts and a T-shirt. It seemed he'd planned on talking to her through the closed door, and she supposed she should have left things that way, with doors firmly closed between them.

But the look in his eyes as they raked over her body in her pretty, white nightgown made her happy that she'd opened this one door. The power of speech seemed to have deserted him completely.

"Going out?" she asked, fighting the urge to cover herself up.

He nodded. "I'm not sure if I'm…ready to sleep. I thought I'd go for a run. I didn't want you to worry if you heard me coming in later or if you came to find me and I was gone."

He wanted to escape, he meant. It gave her a wicked, little thrill.

"Running away?" she asked.

"Maybe," he said.

Oh, he didn't like that. She didn't think he'd ever run from anyone but her.

She took a deep breath. He watched her breasts rise and fall. It was the first time she'd ever felt like she truly had any power over him, and she liked it. She liked it a lot. Could she manage to lose another gown in front of him?

Surely before their honeymoon was over, she could.

Cathie stood up on her toes and brushed a soft kiss against his cheek. He stood rigid at the brief contact. "Well, I'll be right here. Just in case you need me."

Hell, yes, he was running away.

He went out to the beach, wondering how in the world he'd ever thought this would be simple? That he could live with her and not want her or not let her see that he wanted her? He'd known that would be an issue, but thought he could handle it, for her sake and for her baby's. But he'd never thought about her wanting him and coming after him so blatantly.

What was she thinking? Matt wanted to wring her pretty neck.

He told himself she didn't even know what she was asking for. But she was pregnant with someone else's baby. She wasn't quite as innocent as the girl he'd known.

And she wasn't a girl anymore.

The feeling of that delicately soft skin at the side of her breast, his hand on that spot, the lush sweetness of her body cradling his, the sight of her in the thin silk of her nightgown...

And he was the one arguing against this?

Obviously, she'd managed to obliterate every bit of common sense in his body. All with a kiss or two, a dress that was falling down and a nightgown made for a virginally innocent bride.

She was pregnant, but he'd bet money on the fact that she was still innocent, that the idiot she hooked up with had been a lousy, selfish lover. She just didn't handle herself like a woman who knew her way around a man's body or one who was that comfortable with her own half-dressed body in front of a man.

Not that she should be. Not Cathie.

Not that she should ever be married to him, either, but she was, and he was worried that the next time he saw her, she'd just peel off her clothes and dare him not to take her to bed.

What the hell was he supposed to do with her now?

Share a house with her for three years and never touch her?

Or anyone else?

Like *that* was going to happen.

Cathie could have sworn five minutes hadn't passed before she heard a key in the door and then heard Matt come inside. That was odd. She was rolling over to look at the bedside clock when her bedroom door opened and there he was, looking like a madman.

"You've got to listen to me about this. You've got to know this is not the way things are supposed to be," he insisted. "You know what I am. I'm an incompetent car thief, a street kid, a wild one with a no-account father and drunk for a mother, a kid who wasn't supposed to amount to anything—"

"That's not who you are." Cathie sat up in the bed, fighting the urge to pull the covers to her chin. "That's what you used to be and what you came from." And she'd loved him, even then.

"And you. Everything was supposed to go right for you, Cathie. You were supposed to do everything right—"

"I know. I didn't."

"Including staying the hell away from me."

"I tried, Matt. I really did," she said, easing over to the side of the bed, letting her feet fall to the floor and abandoning the covers.

"If anybody was going to seduce you and then walk away from you—I would have bet money it would have been me. And I would have walked sooner or later, Cathie. And I would have broken your heart."

"But you didn't. Somebody else took care of that for you."

"It should have been me," he said, taking three steps across the room until he was standing by her bed, looking down at her. "Not to break your heart. I never wanted to do that. But I wanted you. I wanted to be the first man who ever touched you."

"I wish you had been." She reached out a hand and let it rest, palm flat, on his abdomen, the muscles jumping and tensing beneath her hand. "You'd have been much more careful with me."

He looked down at that hand on his body, but he didn't move away. "I swear, I could strangle the guy. I still might."

"Matt, he doesn't matter anymore."

She dared to raise his shirt ever so slightly, then touched her lips to the tanned skin she'd uncovered at his waist, because she wasn't letting him go now and it didn't seem so intimidating to touch him here.

His body stirred, the running shorts leaving little to the imagination, and she wanted to touch him there, too, but didn't quite have the courage. Let him try to resist her now.

"You don't owe me anything," he said. "And even if you did…you don't owe it to any man to have sex with him."

"It's not about that, Matt." She got both hands under his shirt and let them glide up and over all those lovely muscles, the dents and swells of his hard body, the little peaks of his nipples. It was so nice to finally be able to touch him.

He caught her hands and stilled them. "I'm afraid

you won't be able to keep your heart out of this, and I swore I would never hurt you.''

''I know what we agreed to, and I've learned to be more careful with my heart these days,'' she said. No time left for any shred of pride, she added, ''And I've always wanted to be with you.''

She thought about kissing her way up to his own heart. She'd like that, placing kisses above his heart. She started at his belly, following the thin line of hair up the center of his chest. His breathing was positively ragged and leaning into him this way, she could feel how ready he was for this, thrilled to the knowledge that he wanted her this way.

''Always?'' he said, his hand in her hair, holding her mouth to him.

''For as long as I've known what it was to want a man,'' she confessed, her whole body tingling with need. ''We could spend all kinds of time analyzing this to death, Matt, and trying to figure out how we ended up here and why. But it doesn't really matter, does it? This is where we are, and it's supposed to last a long time, and I just keep thinking, I want you to be with me. For as long as we're together, Matt. Be with me.''

He moaned in answer. She got one of her hands free and slid it down his body until she had the swollen length of him in her hand through his clothes and rubbed up and down. His entire body surged forward for an instant and then back, thrusting into her open hand.

Maybe she was meant to be a wanton woman after all.

''You'll regret it,'' he said raggedly.

"No, I won't."

He reached back and in one smooth motion, pulled his shirt over his head and threw it across the room. He stepped out of his shoes, tugged off his socks and stood there, maybe debating whether to strip completely.

She put her hand on him again, rubbing up and down through his clothes. He closed his eyes and groaned, then caught her by the arms and lifted her to him. His mouth landed on hers and he tucked every inch of her against every impressive inch of him. He gave her a kiss that could have had a woman melting into a puddle at his feet, one that went on and on, told her exactly what he intended to do with her.

She wrapped her arms around him and held on for dear life. "Tell me what to do," she murmured, when they came up for air. "I don't always know what to do."

"You're doing just fine," he said, the low, desperate quality to his voice convincing her that she was.

He palmed her hips, hiked her up a half an inch higher and more firmly against him. His body was so lean and so hard. Everywhere. She clutched at the muscles in his shoulders, his arms, his back, wishing she could slip completely inside of him and never have to leave.

She felt like that's what he'd done to her—gotten inside, all the way down to her soul, and just never left. She'd tried and tried to forget him, to tell herself it was hopeless, that he simply didn't want her. But he did.

They stood there necking like desperate teenagers, and she thought for a moment of that night so long ago when she'd managed to get herself alone with him late at night in her father's pickup, on a pretty hillside overlooking a mountain lake.

It had been like this, just as desperate, except they'd both had all their clothes on and had been lying in the bed of the pickup. She still remembered looking up at the stars, once he'd pulled away from her and sworn that he didn't want her. That he was a man who didn't intend to stop, when he got a woman flat on her back, and he didn't have any trouble getting what he wanted. And it had all been for show. He'd wanted her. His conscience just hadn't let him have her back then.

"Oh, Matt." She'd been so miserable for so many years.

He lifted his head and just breathed for a minute. Took her face in his hand and kissed her softly, sweetly. "Too fast?"

"No."

"All you have to do is say so. Too slow. Too fast. Too much. Not enough. Anything at all. Just tell me. I'll take care of it. I'll—" He broke off.

"What?"

"I was going to say I'll take care of everything, but I don't have a condom."

"Well, it's not like you're going to get me pregnant."

"I'm not going to give you anything, either," he said. "I'm very, very careful."

"And I made the obstetrician do all sorts of tests, just to make sure. It's…all I have is the baby."

He eased away from her, far enough to get his hand in between them, over the slight mound of her belly.

"What about that? I don't want to hurt you. Or the baby."

"The baby will be just fine. The doctor offered that information on her own."

He took her mouth again, more gently this time, lingering, teasing. "Then I guess we don't have anything to worry about."

"No, we don't."

His hands skimmed down her arms, taking down the straps of her gown, and his mouth made a leisurely journey to her neck and her shoulders, along the neckline of her gown.

"It's so pretty. *You* are so pretty," he said, his hand skimming over one of her breasts. "It makes me almost afraid to touch you."

He stood for a minute, just looking at her. The gown was caught on her breasts, barely. He left it hanging, using his mouth and his tongue as if he might need to memorize the entire shape and weight of what he'd managed to uncover of her breasts.

She clutched at him, thinking her legs were going to give out any minute, and that if he didn't get his mouth or his hand over her nipple soon, she was going to have to beg. His breath skimmed across one nipple, and it was like someone had wound a coil inside of her entire body even tighter.

She wanted him there and between her legs and deep inside of her body. She wanted him on top of her, holding her tight and straining to get closer, and she didn't want to ever have to let go.

"Matt, please."

"I will. Promise."

"Soon?"

"Soon."

He took her nipple through the thin silk of her gown and, if possible, the touch was even more erotic.

She whimpered and clutched at his hair.

How much could a woman truly want a man? There had to be some limit. What happened when she reached it? When she couldn't stand it anymore and all the sensations got to be too much?

She'd beg, she supposed.

He'd said all she had to do was ask, and he'd grant her every wish.

"I don't know if I can stand it," she said.

"Because you like it so much?"

"Yes."

"You can." And he went right on doing what he was doing.

Her body throbbed and throbbed, everything going tighter and tighter. His body was rocking against hers in the most arousing way. It would be like this, later, when he was finally inside of her. It would be just like this.

"Matt?" she said urgently. "I don't...well...I think I'm..."

Gently, he pushed her back onto the bed and followed her down, still not pulling the gown from her body, just pushing a hand up beneath the long skirt. Then he was back, teasing her breast at first, and then sucking hard through her gown. His hand teased ever so lightly at the heat between her legs.

Honestly, he barely touched her.

That was all it took.

She cried out, and then clamped a hand over her mouth to stifle the sound.

''It's all right,'' he said, still working over her breast. ''There's no one to hear but me, and I want to hear it, Cath. Just trust me. And let go.''

She cried out again, her body taking over. She couldn't have stopped if she'd tried. It scared her a little and embarrassed her, later, when she thought about it. Because he'd barely touched her, and she was gone.

He drove her on, up and over, her body going tighter and tighter like a spring, and then she took off and could have sworn she was floating. All she could do was lay there and breathe.

He finally pushed the gown down with his mouth and stroked her breasts ever so delicately with his lips, kissing the little beads of sweat off her breastbone. She shivered and held onto him, waiting until she could feel the bed beneath her back and knew she was back on the ground.

When he lifted his head, there was a hard stamp of pure satisfaction on his handsome face, and she knew what was coming out of his mouth next.

Embarrassed, she said, ''I know what you're about to ask me, and I'm not saying a word—''

''Cathie, I don't have to ask.''

If she hadn't been so satisfied, she'd have smacked him. She didn't think she'd ever seen him look so sure of himself in his life.

Okay, so he was good at this. That wasn't exactly a revelation. Although, what he made her feel certainly was, and if he could take satisfaction in that, he was welcome to it. She'd thought she'd known what one of those was, had been pretty sure she'd had one. But it hadn't been like that. Nothing had ever been like that. And he knew it.

He stretched out beside her, rolling her up onto her side, beginning again to build on the heat simmering inside of her.

She felt as if they'd come a thousand miles already and wondered how much farther he could possibly take her. But it was a long, long time before he stripped off the rest of his clothes and settled himself ever-so-carefully on top of her.

She'd cried both in satisfaction and frustration by the time he did, felt absolutely powerless against the sensations he aroused in her. His body was a wonder. Absolutely beautiful and big and powerful, and the way he moved against her, the way they fit together…it was like the universe had shifted and made a place just for her, and it was with him.

He'd made this just for her, just about pleasing her, showing her the way it would have been if he'd been her very first lover. But she wasn't going to beat herself up about that. Not now that he was here. Not when her body was absolutely aching for him.

He moved carefully, keeping most of his weight on his powerful arms. She felt him moving at the opening of her body, rocking ever so gently against her, pushing a little more inside with every stroke.

She wanted him so bad she'd taken to begging. *Please, please, please* over and over again.

"I'm there, Cathie. I'm right there. Tell me if anything hurts."

"Nothing hurts."

She lifted her hips, meeting his tiny thrust with one of her own. He slid just a bit farther, her body working to accommodate him. She could feel little shivery contractions, and the strength in his arms and his back, in his hips and his legs. In every bit of him.

His forehead came down to rest on hers. He kissed her temple. "I hurt. I ache."

"What can I do?" Instinctively, she let her legs fall open even more and pushed up and against him.

He groaned. "That. Do that."

She swiveled her hips, taking him inch by inch, wishing she could make him as crazy as he made her.

He came down on his elbows, so that their bodies were brushing against each other from head to toe, and let her set the pace, finally bringing himself fully inside of her. And with him, it was simply a beautiful thing, all-encompassing and overwhelming and exhausting.

She cried out and sank her nails into his hips and tears seeped from the corners of her eyes. Satisfaction came over her in deep, powerful waves, her body clutching his.

She wasn't sure she had the power to do that to him, but finally that iron control of his broke, and he nearly crushed her to him, thrusting long and hard, crying out himself, shuddering against her.

His face was next to hers, their cheeks pressed together, his mouth on hers. She held him so tight, and felt like he'd taken her completely out of this world, into a place she'd never imagined.

"Oh, Matt."

It was all she could do not to tell him she'd been in love with him for most of her life and probably would be forever.

He went to pull away, gazing down at her. "You okay?"

"Much better than that."

"You sure? I got a little carried away, there at the end."

"I know." She grinned, fighting the urge to ask if it could possibly always be like that for him, wanting to know that what they shared was something very, very special.

Surely it was.

He eased his weight off her by edging ever so slightly to one side, so he wasn't really leaving her. Not that she would have let him. Not yet.

"I don't ever want you to move," she said.

"You will. I'll make sure of it."

He said it with a slow, satisfied smile that sent pure joy rushing through her. She didn't think she'd ever seen Matt this relaxed or this happy, knew she'd never felt this good herself.

She took his face in her hands and kissed him one more time, saying with her body what she couldn't put into words. That she loved him.

He eased off her, pulled the covers up over her shoulders and then stretched out flat on the bed beside her, holding out his arms to her.

She snuggled against him, his arms locked around her, and they both sank into the pillowy softness of the bed.

Contentment like she'd never known washed over her, and she drifted into sleep, having the sweetest dream of her life.

Chapter Seven

Matt woke once again with an armful of woman. Smooth, sweet-smelling, bare skin and soft curves, her breath stirring across his chest, her body pressed against his side.

He'd been here before, but not like this.

Not with Cathie.

Her father's face flashed through his memory. All four of her brothers'. Mary's. Cathie's when she was much younger and so determined to save him, and he groaned.

How had he ended up here? How had she?

He had sworn to her entire family and to himself that he would never, ever hurt her. He never wanted anything in this world to hurt her, and if he could have protected her that way, he would have.

And now he was married to her, kind of, and in her

bed, and no amount of guilt was going to be able to make him leave her alone now that he'd had her.

She stirred in his arms, stretching a bit and then going still, probably once she realized she wasn't alone. She leaned back and tilted her head up to his, grimacing as she forced open her eyes and stared at him.

He stared right back, not at all sure what kind of reaction he'd get from her this morning or where they'd go from here. He hadn't been a part of a lot of morning-after scenes. He tended not to stay that long, even when he got into a regular relationship with a woman. Or as regular as his relationships got.

So he had no idea what to expect from a morning-after with Cathie.

"I might have to pinch you," she said.

"What?"

"You know…to see if you're real."

"Be my guest."

She pinched a bit of skin on his belly. Or tried to. Everything in him stirred at her touch. He wanted her again, already, had wanted more of her last night but hadn't wanted to hurt her or the baby. He'd forgotten all about the baby there in the end. And she'd been exhausted.

So she'd slept, and he'd worried and felt guilty and thought about how incredible it was to sink into this pillowy-soft bed with her wrapped around him and wondered what the morning would bring. And wanted her some more.

"You don't pinch very well, but the muscles feel familiar," she said, her palm stretched out flat, low on his abdomen. "I think you did spend the night in my bed."

"I did," he admitted.

"Well, do you have to look so grim about it? I thought you liked it." She rolled over onto her side, pulling covers up and over her pretty curves, staring at him with the bluest, most innocent eyes he'd ever seen.

Her hair was in disarray, and he tucked a strand behind one ear. Maybe he had to touch her, too, to make sure this was real. He'd had his hands in those silken locks last night, holding her to him by a handful of her hair, brushing it away from her face, so he could get to her mouth.

"I liked it," he said. "A lot."

"So, what is this? You're just not a morning person?" she tried. "Because you used to be."

"Cathie, what are we going to do?"

She thought about it for a minute and then said, in all seriousness, "Find breakfast?"

He frowned at her.

"What else do we need to do?" she asked. "I mean, if you really have to worry some more and analyze everything and tell me how things are supposed to be, I suppose I can't stop you. But what I'd really like is some tea and toast, to settle my stomach, and then I want to see the island."

Bewildered, he said, "That's it?"

"Well, we never had a problem getting along before. Not until we were wanting each other and not doing anything about it," she reasoned. "So, I was thinking now that we are...doing something about it...maybe we could just go back to being friends. The way we used to be? Friends and lovers? It doesn't have to be any more complicated than that, does it?''

He didn't buy that for a minute. She wasn't made that way. But she was the last person on earth he'd expected to ever end up pregnant and all alone, too. So he supposed that maybe—just maybe—in a universe where she could end up that way, she could also end up with him, temporarily. That he wouldn't have to worry about her falling in love with him and him making her miserable, because someone else had already done that. Surely she'd learned from that mistake.

''Don't make it any more complicated than it has to be, Matt,'' she said. ''We're going to be together, and I know exactly why. I won't forget. But we can make it a good time, can't we?''

Again, this was not her. Not her at all. She was not a good-time girl.

Nevertheless, here he was, in a bed that was like a big, puffy cloud, with her. All that bare skin and long, loose hair, the sheet clutched to her chest as she looked at him invitingly from across the stark-white of the sheets.

It was one of the strangest places he'd ever been and the best.

There'd been times in the past few years, when his company had taken off and he'd realized he'd never again have to worry about money or respectability, when he'd felt a sense of pride that bordered on sheer arrogance.

But there'd been something missing.

The happiest times in his life, he'd spent with Cathie.

She'd taught him to laugh, taught him to enjoy the simple pleasures to be had in a summer's day. She'd been sunshine and warmth, trust and hope. She'd shown a faith in him that no one ever had before. She'd tamed him, when he'd thought he was going to turn absolutely wild and live on the streets for the rest of his life, roaming from place to place, never knowing what a home was.

She'd given him all that, and, dammit, life should have been a breeze for her.

She never should have ended up in his bed.

"Just let it be, Matt," she said, her hand coming to rest on his chest, near the vicinity of his battered heart. "We were good together once. We can be like that again."

It was indeed that easy to be with her, to slip back into their old, familiar friendship, one he'd missed so much over the years.

Cathie had a way of finding delight in anything new, especially new places. He loved being able to show her the island, which truly was beautiful. He ran on the beach in the mornings, and she walked, meeting him for the last mile of his cool-down, the two of them walking back to their bungalow together. They usually managed to get in some sight-seeing in the mornings. They went horseback riding through the lush hillsides, water-skiing, sailing, snorkeling. Anything she wanted.

Afternoons, they spent in bed.

They'd get dressed and have dinner at the hotel, maybe go dancing until he couldn't stand it anymore and hustled her back to the bungalow.

He wanted her indecently often, having to keep reminding himself that she was pregnant, and that he needed to be careful with her. That she needed to rest.

She came into his arms eagerly, sometimes a bit shyly, with an innocence, an honesty and openness he'd never known. He kept waiting for the need he had for her to ease, for the urgency to fade away, but it hadn't.

They'd only been scheduled to stay for ten days, but he found he didn't want to leave and neither did she. So he managed to extend the trip to fourteen days, for once not thinking about all he should be doing at the office. Nothing about responsibilities or duties or obligations. Just what he wanted, which was more time here with her.

On their next-to-last day, she pleaded fatigue one morning and told him all she really wanted to do was lie in the sun, and sent him off to play golf, which he'd only done once on the entire trip. She'd come with him then. He'd spent more time laughing at her efforts to play than thinking about his game, couldn't have even said what he shot that day, hadn't cared.

Truthfully, he didn't care that next-to-last day, either.

He looked at the trees and the green grass, the turquoise-blue ocean and the puffy clouds overhead that reminded them of their bed at the bungalow. He'd never forget that bed.

Or the time he'd spent in it with her.

He didn't even finish the round. Just quit playing on the fourteenth green without even making his putt.

Time was short. He wanted to be with her, and there'd been damned few times in his life when it had been possible to simply have what he wanted. Once the work he'd done had made it possible, there'd been too few times when he'd allowed himself that luxury. Discipline and hard work had always taken precedence, and now, for once, it wasn't.

He got to the bungalow and went room-to-room, looking for her but not finding her. Maybe she was at the beach. He went out the back door and down to the water, not seeing her, telling himself not to worry. She wouldn't have gone anywhere.

Coming back, he almost missed her.

The trees and the foliage closed in around the tiny backyard of the bungalow, creating something of a courtyard, open in the back to the ocean. Off to the side in the shade, was a generous-sized wooden lounge chair with a pretty, bright yellow cushion.

Cathie was stretched out on her stomach, sleeping maybe.

Her entire body was bare, save for the tiny bottom of an honest-to-goodness string bikini. Two little scraps of flowery material held together by strings, tied at either side of her hips.

He stood there taking in the broad expanse of bare skin, which had turned a pale, pale pink in the sun. Long legs, the swell of her bottom, the little dent at the base of her spine, the soft curves of her breasts pressed against the cushions, her arms stretched out above her head, hands dangling off the end of the lounge chair, her hair spread out across her back and her arms.

He must have made some kind of sound, giving himself away, because she turned drowsily to him and gave him a lazy smile.

"Back already?"

He nodded.

"Good game?"

He had no idea. "I was wondering if you could help me with something."

"Sure. What is it?"

"I'm looking for my wife."

She grinned then, looking a little more awake, not moving from her spot on the chair. "Matt, I am your wife. Remember?"

"No." He came closer, surveying the space a little more closely. There was no one on the beach, and unless someone came right up to the edge of the bungalow's property and peered into the back corner of their tiny courtyard, they'd never be seen here. He suspected she knew that. "My wife would never sunbathe without her top. She wouldn't wear anything like what you've got on out in public. She's a very good girl. A preacher's daughter."

"Really?"

"Yes."

He started stripping off his clothes. She was beautiful. He wanted her right here, right now, maybe as much as he ever had in his whole life. Which was hard to imagine, given how many times he'd made love to her on this island in the past thirteen days.

She still hadn't moved. He found he didn't want her to.

"What are you going to do with her, when you find her?" she asked.

Witch.

Surely she'd bewitched him.

"I'm going to do this," he said, kneeling beside her

chair, his hand skimming up the back of one thigh, from the back of her knee to the enticing curve of her bottom.

''Mmmm. That's nice.''

Nice? He'd show her nice.

His mouth settled at the back of one of her knees. She whimpered, her whole body going tense. Good. So he wasn't the only one.

He made a slow journey with his mouth from the back of her knees to her bottom, nibbling on all the pretty, sun-warmed skin, undoing the ties at either side of that silly excuse for a bathing suit but leaving the triangular scraps of material in place.

He nibbled his way around the mounds of her hips, trailing along the now bare skin of her thighs and onto her back, settling himself on the chair on top of her. His hands worked their way up her back, softly, teasing her, liking the way her body writhed beneath his.

''Matt, please,'' she said.

''Please what?''

''I want to kiss you, too. I want to touch you.''

''In a minute,'' he said. ''I'm not done yet.''

It was like a veritable feast of skin awaiting him, and he wanted his mouth on every bit of it. There was a raging heat inside of him that he ruthlessly denied, thinking he might never see her like this again, because she was shy and she'd set him up for this, but it wouldn't have been easy for her, outside in broad daylight.

She probably thought they'd end up inside in their bed, and they would. Just not yet. He wanted her here first.

His mouth settled into that little notch near the bottom of her spine. Her entire body came up off the chair, but there was nowhere for her to go. He had her pinned down.

"That's good?" he asked, doing it again.

"Yes."

He kissed her back some more. It was like going on a treasure hunt, finding some new, wonderfully responsive spot on her body.

She moved restlessly beneath him. He stayed where he was, playing with her back, his hands gliding up to find the outer curves of her pretty breasts.

Slowly, slowly, he made his way up her spine to her neck. She had the softest skin on her neck, and there was a spot there...

She groaned again. He settled himself more fully on top of her, his erection settling into the sweet curves of her bottom. She wriggled against him, the pressure exquisite, and he sank his teeth into that spot on her neck that drove her wild.

He'd meant to make it last even longer. To peel off that silly excuse for a swimsuit and flip her over and start from her toes and work his way up the front of her body this time. Letting her lie there with the sun on her bare breasts and wait until he got to them and to her mouth, until he finally got inside of her.

But he didn't have it in him to wait that long. So he stretched out beside her and pulled her into his arms.

"Matt?" she protested.

"No one's going to see. It's just us and the birds and the sky, and they don't care."

He kissed her long and hard, thought as best he could about how he wanted to do this, and finally settled for rolling onto his back and pulling her on top of him. He kissed her one more time and then eased her thighs apart, groaning at the heat he found there.

She wanted him, too. There was no denying it.

He palmed her hips, drawing her to him, slipping barely inside. She cried out at the first intimate touch and then bit her lip to keep from making another sound.

"Cathie, there's no one to hear, either. Except me." And he liked all those little sounds she made. The surprise and the urgency, all the things she couldn't hold back.

Her body stretched and gave, and he slipped inside, pulling her down on top of him. There was heat, a rich, moist heat, and her body had a way of grabbing onto his and holding him there, that made him crazy, too. The pressure was exquisite.

He took her by the arms and pushed her up. She didn't understand at first, and he somehow managed to bite back a smile. Her innocence was a constant surprise and a pleasure he'd never anticipated enjoying so much.

"Like this," he said, settling her firmly on top of him.

She groaned, as her new position took him more deeply inside of her, and then she wriggled her hips, and he nearly lost it right there.

The sun was going down. It was somewhere behind her head, and the light made her hair and her skin shine like burnt gold. Her body was toned and slender, and he couldn't take his eyes off her.

His hands slid up her nearly flat stomach. He cupped her breasts, watching the play of his hands on her, watching everything, the sight of her nearly undoing him.

She'd figured out what to do now, figured out the power this position gave her, and she used it ruthlessly, moving ever so slightly and so tightly against him, rocking back and forth, holding him so deeply inside of her.

His hands bit into her hips. He feared he'd leave marks on her. And his body bucked up, going deeper and deeper. She cried out, her body tightening around him. He watched her face, watched the pleasure come over her, and when she finally collapsed in his arms, he thrust inside of her once more, then again, and then the whole world seemed to come apart.

He could swear he felt it shift and shake beneath him. Everything in the whole, wide world.

He cried out himself, crushing her to him, kissing her again and again and again, until every muscle in his body went slack, and they lay there in a tangle of arms and legs and bare skin, simply unable to move.

Cathie returned from her honeymoon in a daze, hardly even sure of her own name, her brain was so scrambled from the sheer pleasure of the time they'd spent together. She felt foolish and naive and completely out of her league, hadn't even known that kind of satisfaction and need existed in this world. As much as she'd ever wanted Matt...she just hadn't known.

And he knew it.

She sighed and leaned back in her wide, leather seat in the first-class cabin.

"You okay?" Matt, from the seat beside her, took her hand in his.

She nodded. "Just…" Foolish? Embarrassed? Uncertain? She felt all of those things. And one more. Regrets. "I don't want to leave."

He gave her an honest-to-goodness grin, looking more relaxed than she'd seen him in years. Was this what wild sex in broad daylight in a courtyard did to a man? Or was it something more?

He seemed so happy.

Would they be able to hang onto those feelings, once they were back home? Or was this just the look of a man who was thoroughly relaxed after two weeks on a beach in the middle of a North Carolina winter?

"We'll come back," he said. "If I can find the time, before the baby comes."

Her heart gave a little lurch, thinking that he wanted to go back, thinking of how happy he'd seemed there, wondering if she could make him that happy day to day, back home.

Surely if he could feel like that, he'd never want her or the baby to leave. He'd never want those feelings to stop.

"I'd like that," she said, thinking that maybe she did know what to do after all to make her marriage work.

She'd just love him. Completely. Without reservation. As she would if they'd gone into this marriage for real, and he knew that she truly loved him and always had. She'd show him how their lives together could be and hope that he wanted it without any time limit at all, that he could love her as much as she loved him.

They got back to North Carolina shortly after three in the afternoon, grumbling halfheartedly about the cold after the bright sunshine they'd left behind.

He drove into the gated subdivision he called home, watching Cathie's face as she took in the large, brick homes and the wide, lush lawns. The houses looked solid and absolutely respectable, and they were expensive. One more way of saying he'd arrived. Cathie would probably take one look inside and see right through his motives, but it was too late to do anything about it now.

He pulled into his driveway, hit a button in the car to open the three-car garage and parked inside. Cathie was drowsy. She didn't stir until he opened her car door. He had the ridiculous urge to carry her over the threshold, and then thought, *Why not?*

"Hang on," he said, lifting her into his arms.

"Matt?" She finally opened her eyes. "What are you doing?"

"You are the bride, right?"

"Yes," she said, her arms clasped around his shoulders.

"This is the last wedding tradition I know about. So if there's anything else, you'll have to let me know. I'd hate to miss anything."

"I think we hit all the high points," she said, laughing.

They certainly had on the honeymoon. But then, people claimed honeymoons never lasted.

Matt carried her around to the front walkway, so they could go in the front door. It didn't seem right to go in through the garage.

"Wow!" She gazed up at it. "Do you think the two of us will fit in this house?"

"I think we'll manage," he claimed.

"Did you buy the biggest house you could find?"

"What if I did?" he said, thinking they might as well get that over and done with. He got to the front door and frowned. "How's a guy supposed to open the door with arms full of bride?"

Cathie laughed again. It was worth making the gesture to hear her laugh.

"Here." He turned her toward the state-of-the-art digital lock. "You open it. The code's your parents' phone number."

"Really?"

He shrugged. "Easy to remember and hardly anyone would connect it to me now."

She unlocked the door and pushed it open. He carried her inside and said, "Welcome home, Mrs. Monroe."

She kissed him softly on the lips, her face lingering near his. "Thank you."

He didn't quite know what to say, so he kissed her again and again. Kicked the door closed and thought about carrying her upstairs to his bed or to the big sofa in the family room. Cathie gave him every indication that she'd have no problem with either of those options.

He was thinking about it when the phone rang. He hadn't intended to answer, but he'd been away from his office for more than two weeks.

He kissed her again. The phone at the house stopped ringing, but not five seconds later, his cell phone started. Matt lifted his head and set her on her feet.

"Sorry," he said, reaching for the phone. "I have a feeling this is the office."

She stood waiting while he took the call. As he expected, they had a problem he needed to fix.

"If you can drag yourself away from your wife," Brenda Masterson, his assistant, said.

"What does that mean?" he asked.

"You haven't managed to stay out of this office for two straight days, much less two and a half weeks, since I came to work for you six years ago. Mrs. Monroe must be something."

"She is," he said.

"And you two just got back?"

"Not five minutes ago."

Brenda whistled. "She's not gonna be happy about you walking out on her five minutes after you got home."

"Really?"

"Oh, honey. You've got so much to learn about being a married man."

"I'm sure between you and my wife, you can tell me everything I need to know," he said. "I'll be there soon."

Cathie had drifted into the formal living room, which looked a lot like an overstuffed furniture store to him. He could have sworn the room was so big, until the decorator had brought in all this stuff.

"I'm afraid I have to go to the office for a while," he said.

Cathie just looked at him. Not upset. Not surprised. Just waiting.

"Tell me how to do this, Cathie. Because I just don't know."

"Do what?"

"This, uh…marriage thing."

She shook her head, smiled a bit. "We're doing all right so far, aren't we?"

He nodded. Things had been just fine.

"I think we can make it up as we go along. I don't want to get in your way. Or make things difficult for you. I just... I want you to be happy, Matt."

"I want you to be happy, too," he said.

"So, we'll just see how it goes?"

"Okay. I don't know how long I'll be, but...let me give you the grand tour. Your things should be here, somewhere."

They walked quickly through the house, and she managed not to frown. He saw it, as she must see it, a place that looked like a decorator had done it and no one had moved in yet. Except for his office at the back of the house, the weights set up in the basement and a few personal items in his bedroom.

"Okay, I wrote a check and gave the woman carte blanche," he finally said. "Can you fix it?"

She frowned. "That depends. What do you want done with it?"

"Make it look like someone lives here?"

"I'm afraid the trick to that is having someone actually live here, Matt."

"I live here."

"But you're never here, right? And being in the office downstairs and sleeping don't count."

"So, you'll live here. Make it look like you live here."

"No. It's yours. It should be what you want it to be."

"Make it look like what you'd want it to be," he said. "That'll be fine."

He wanted to tell her to make it stop looking empty, stop feeling empty, but that was more than he was ready to reveal even to her, although, she probably knew that, too.

"I have to go," he said, wondering what a fake husband who happened to be sleeping with his wife did at a moment like this?

She stood across the bedroom that had never really felt like his, running her hand along the bed. "My things are in the room down the hall."

"I know," he said carefully. When he'd had them put there, he hadn't anticipated the kind of honeymoon they'd had. "You can have any room you like."

Looking as tentative as he felt, she said, "This one?"

He nodded, holding her gaze, realizing only then how much he wanted her here every night when he went to sleep and every morning when he woke up.

He held his breath until she said, "Can we share?"

"That would work for me." And then, before he tumbled her onto the bed and christened their new room, he turned away and said, "I may be late. Make yourself at home."

They gave him six kinds of hell at the office. For being gone so long. For not even calling to check in. For coming back to the office so soon after he and Cathie returned. He took it and said as little as possible, surprised at how many people wished him well and congratulated him. He wasn't one to bring his personal life into the office, although he tried to be understanding when other people had personal issues distracting them or keeping them away. They were a tight-knit group. He expected a lot from them and they gave it. He tried to be understanding in return.

He had a mountain of e-mail and faxes to deal with, a long list of people who claimed they had to see him right away, and one major crisis with one of his biggest customers, whose system had somehow been hacked into early this morning. He did what had to be done and four hours later was on his way out of the office when Jim Dornen, his attorney, walked in, grinning and holding out his hand.

"You really did it? You got married?" Jim asked.

Matt took his hand. "I did."

Three times divorced himself, Jim said, "Tell me you got a prenup?"

"No."

"Good God, are you nuts? Do you remember what you're worth? What this company's worth?"

"Not exactly. I haven't seen a stock quote in two and a half weeks. Why?"

Jim rolled his eyes. "She'll kill us. You'll walk away from her one day, or even worse, she'll leave you, and she'll kill us in the divorce settlement."

Matt grinned. "No, she won't."

"Hey, if I had a nickel for every fool who's said that to me—"

"You don't know her, Jim."

"And you think you do?"

"Since she was eight years old," he said.

"Eight?"

Matt nodded.

"You never said a word…"

Matt shrugged. What could he say?

"She must be something," Jim said. "Still, you can

do an agreement like a prenup after the wedding. It's just as binding. All you have to do is get her to sign.''

''No,'' Matt said.

''I'll take care of it. I've handled things like this before. She'll be fine with it.''

''No,'' Matt said again, more forcefully this time. ''No papers. No agreement. Nothing. Don't say a word to her. Do you understand?'' It was a tone he seldom took with anyone. But he meant it. He didn't want any misunderstandings about this.

Jim backed off, giving him an even odder look. ''Okay. If that's what you want.''

''No.'' It just hit him that he was married, and a man had to be prepared, just in case. She and the baby deserved that. ''Actually, we need to take care of something.''

''Now you're talkin', buddy.''

''Life insurance beneficiary. My will. Company stock and how it's handled. That stuff will have to be updated.''

Jim groaned and looked like he was about to make another plea.

''But not tonight,'' Matt said. ''Tonight, I'm going home to my wife.''

He pulled up to a house with light coming from deep inside. Opened the door to find the place smelling heavenly, like tomatoes and spices. In the kitchen, peering over a steaming pot on the stove, was his wife.

He found he liked thinking of her that way.

She looked up and gave him a mischievous look. ''Tough day at the office, dear?''

He nodded.

"Hungry?"

"Yes." He'd forgotten what a good cook she was, and she looked so cute in the middle of his big, mostly empty kitchen, so domesticated. She was barefoot, her toenails nearly the same soft pink of her skin. No matter how much sun she got, she never tanned. Just turned pink. A pair of jeans clung to the sweet curves of her bottom. A little pink sweater dipped low between her breasts, but he had to look down the little, red apron she wore to see that. He'd caught her licking the big spoon she'd used to stir the sauce.

"Gonna bring me my slippers and the paper, dear?"

She put down the spoon and untied her apron strings, looking relaxed and happy and just right, here in this room waiting for him. "Do you own a pair of slippers?"

"Come to think of it, I don't."

"I suppose I could buy you some, for moments like this."

"Why don't you just feed me instead?"

She did. It was spaghetti, her grandmother's recipe. He'd forgotten how good that was, but she'd remembered it had always been one of his favorites. They sat at the tiny table in the corner of the kitchen, just the two of them. It was quiet and comfortable. They lingered there, the conversation easy, his brain trying to get a handle on this new reality of his.

Had he really thought so little was going to change?

They finished dinner. She went to clean up, but he stopped her, telling her he had a cleaning lady who came in twice a week, that she would take care of it. Cathie claimed he was spoiled rotten if he couldn't put his own dishes in the dishwasher, and he had to defend himself and say he did, when he ate here, which wasn't often. He had a feeling he would from now on.

She yawned as they finished, and he said, "You're worn out. You have classes tomorrow?"

"Bright and early. I need to get to bed."

He nodded, thinking he had work to do, things to catch up on. That it was surely indecent how much he wanted her, how, as much as she satisfied him, afterward he seemed to only want her more.

She headed for the stairs and he followed her up, telling himself he'd move her things into his room and nothing else. That she was pregnant and tired and he should be able to exercise some control over himself.

He lugged boxes and suitcases.

She went into his bathroom and came out in that pretty, white thing she'd worn on their wedding night. A cloud of steam billowed out behind her and the scent she wore wafted his way.

She walked over to him and got up on her tiptoes to kiss him softly and tell him good-night. When she went to pull away, he put his hands on her arms to stop her, looking down into her pretty blue eyes, having no idea what to say.

Reading his mind, something she seemed to do with alarming regularity, she said, "Whatever you want it to be, Matt."

Just like that?

He honestly didn't think there'd been a time in his life when he thought about doing exactly what he'd wanted or trying to figure out what would make him happy or how that would feel.

Like this, he thought, touching her through the pretty, white silk gown. It would feel like this.

"What did you think of the cloud mattress on the bed at the bungalow?" he asked, his mouth teasing the tender skin at her neck.

"I liked it."

"Me, too." Sinking into it would always make him think of the sheer pleasure of sinking into her warm, welcoming arms. "I was thinking I might find us one for this bed."

Chapter Eight

He ordered a cloud mattress for the master bedroom and enjoyed the purchase more than anything he'd ever bought before. She did, too. He also bought her a new car, a little Mercedes SUV, which she gave him a hard time about accepting. He told her he wanted her and the baby to be safe, and that his wife couldn't very well drive a thirty-year-old, beat-up, broken-down VW bug while he drove a Mercedes. *What would people think?* She finally took the keys and stopped complaining.

She started classes, napped nearly every afternoon, and was at home, waiting for him, every night when he got there. She fed him delicious food and rubbed his shoulders and made him laugh. Made no demands upon him, never complained, never argued.

He made the mistake of mentioning that to Jim,

when they were out of town on a business trip in February, and Jim said, "This is not a normal marriage."

"No, it's not," he agreed.

"Hell, it's only been six weeks. Give it time."

Which reminded Matt of the time. Nearly seven. They had reservations for dinner with their new clients. "We should get going."

"Need to check in with the little woman first?"

Matt glared at him. He would call. Not because he needed to hear her voice or anything like that or because she'd ever expect him to check in with her on a regular basis. Just…because. To make sure she was okay. He didn't like her being all alone in that big, expensive house, an attitude she found ridiculous, pointing out that she'd lived in a terrible neighborhood, in an apartment that was far less secure, before and nothing had happened. He still checked up on her.

"I'll call when we get back," he said.

Jim nodded. "Still in that stage where you hate to spend one night away from her?"

Matt nodded toward the door. Who wouldn't *rather* spend the night with a soft, willing woman, than alone in a hotel room on the road? Fabulous sex coupled with the ease of a longtime friendship was proving to be a very nice combination. Cathie's father had always told him life was meant to be shared, not lived alone. Of course, her father meant shared with someone a man loved, and Matt didn't love her. But he liked being with her, and she claimed there was nothing wrong with them simply being together for now, making the most of the time they spent together.

Something in the back of his head—that little part of him that had never truly learned to relax and never really been happy—said there had to be something wrong with it. That it was bound to explode in his face when he least expected it.

For now, he was determined to let himself simply enjoy it.

He rushed the dinner, when they could easily have lingered over coffee and talked through a few more points of their recently cemented agreement with their new clients, but he really didn't care. He liked to meet with new clients personally and assure them that his company would take care of their needs, that if they had a problem, they could come to him. But he was starting to resent the time it took and the travel.

Back in his hotel room, he stripped off his tie and unbuttoned his shirt. Propping the pillows up against the headboard, he stretched out on the bed and picked up the phone to call Cathie.

She said, "Hi," sounding tired, but happy to hear from him.

"Sorry I woke you."

"It's good that you did. I dozed off on the couch, and I would have been stiff and sore in the morning."

"You feel okay?"

"Just tired. I made an appointment with that charity furniture store. They're sending a truck by tomorrow, to clear things out of the rest of the downstairs. I was sorting and rearranging things this afternoon. There's more than I realized that needs to go."

She'd done so much in such a short time. The house no longer looked like a decorator's showroom. He liked it more every day, but that was no reason for her to wear herself out.

"I told you not to do that by yourself. You name

the day you're ready to sort and move the stuff, and I'll send you a couple of guys over. I don't want you moving anything around yourself.''

''I know. I just let the date sneak up on me, and by then, it was too late to ask you to send someone to the house.''

''No, it's not too late. I told you, you can always get me on the road. For anything. Call next time. You're sure you're okay?''

''Yes. I'm just kind of achy all over. I think I may be coming down with the flu. That's all.''

''You're sure?''

''Matt, people get stuffy noses and sore throats all the time.''

He was quiet for a long time, telling himself she was a grown woman, and the doctor had assured him that she was perfectly healthy, and he probably was being ridiculous. She just looked so fragile sometimes, and she was always tired. He didn't care if the doctor thought that was normal for pregnant women. He hadn't ever thought of the toll it takes on a woman's body, to grow a baby inside of her and carry it for nine months.

The baby was still small, but it had made its presence known in her body. Cathie had a tiny, rounded mound in her tummy. So firm and small. He curled his body around hers, sometimes, deep in the night, and let his hand rest on her belly, over the baby, fighting the urge not to tell the baby to behave and not dare give its mother a hard time.

Cathie talked to the baby. He caught her every now and then. Telling the baby she couldn't wait to see it, and that she wasn't having any luck at all picking out names. About the weather or the flowers she'd planted in the garden out back. Telling the baby not to worry about anything, that everything would be okay. He'd missed the beginning of that particular conversation. What was she worrying about? What did she think her baby would be worried about?

"How's Skipper?" he asked.

"Just fine."

That's what he'd taken to calling the baby. Cathie had refused to find out the sex ahead of time, which made it hard to talk about the bossy, little creature inside of her. Matt finally insisted it had to have a name. Since they'd both taken to using the baby as an excuse for anything they wanted to talk the other one into, and Matt was calling it a bossy little thing already, he'd nicknamed the baby Skipper, after Cathie had rejected the Boss, the General and Prez.

So now, it was *Drink your milk. Skipper likes it.*

She claimed Skip liked ice cream more.

Don't you dare haul those plants home from the nursery and install them yourself. Skipper would hate that.

She claimed Skip loved the pretty purplish bushes and all the little flowers.

"Just take care of yourself," Matt said. "And if you do anything else you're not supposed to do, Skip'll tell me."

"Enlisted my baby as your spy?"

"Yes. I'll be home early. We have things to do, remember?"

She didn't know it yet, but they were going shopping for baby things. Tomorrow was Valentine's Day, and he'd been assured by Brenda that with the holiday coming within a few weeks of their wedding, he'd better be ready with some grand gesture of love, otherwise there'd be trouble in his house.

He'd decided filling up Skipper's room would do nicely.

He told Cathie good-night, then got on the phone with the airlines, getting on an earlier flight home. He had some things he had to do at the office tomorrow, but there was no harm in getting them done sooner rather than later, and he could make sure Cathie was feeling okay, and that she got to bed early.

And if she wasn't too tired, he could have her in the clouds.

Yeah, he liked the cloud mattress. And his wife.

He managed to make it home by one o'clock, found a furniture truck backed up to his driveway, and saw two guys carrying out the biggest, ugliest table he'd ever seen. Had that really been in his house?

Then Cathie came out carrying a box. He got out of the car and glared at his wife, taking the box from her hand. "What are you doing?"

"Matt, it's a box. It's not even heavy."

"I don't care," he said, realizing on some level how irrational that sounded and not caring about that, either. She'd been worn-out last night. He put the box down and turned to the moving guys, pulled out his wallet and slipped them both fifty-dollar bills behind her back. "She doesn't lift a thing, understand?"

"Yes, sir," they said.

Cathie turned around and put her hands on her hips. "What did you say?"

"You heard me," he said, thinking if he'd been

really smart, he would have kissed her first, before he'd started arguing. *Oh, well.*

She gave him a look that told him she thought he was being ridiculous, but it wasn't the first time that had happened, and he really didn't care. He was going to take care of her as best he could, even if he made her fighting mad doing it.

"You are the most ridiculous man," she said.

Then he figured out how to get his kiss. He grinned at her. "Happy Valentine's Day, *dear.*" They'd fallen into the habit of calling each other *dear,* just like that, when they fell into some stereotypical husband-and-wife thing. Ever since she'd asked him if he'd had a hard day at the office that first night when he'd come home, and he'd asked her to go fetch his slippers.

She came to him and kissed him, feigning reluctance, but not the irritation. "That's it? Our first Valentine's Day together, and you come home and growl at me?"

"That's it. Honeymoon's over," he claimed, and then she laughed and kissed him for real. He whispered in her ear, "Have you had your afternoon nap?"

"You think we're going from *'The honeymoon's over,'* to the cloud mattress, just like that?"

He played innocent. "Does that mean no?"

She just laughed, but she didn't lift anything else. They dealt with the movers, and he rubbed her back, thinking she needed a real nap and that he should make sure she got it. But she pulled him down to the bed with her, and he made slow, sweet love to her and let her sleep until five before he woke her, mostly just to make sure she was okay.

She sat up a bit, rubbed her back with one hand and insisted that she was.

"Turn over," he ordered, sitting down on the side of the bed.

She did, and he pulled down the sheet, uncovering all the pretty lines of her back and the beginning curves of her luscious bottom. It reminded him of her outside without her top at the bungalow on the island, and he remembered that he wanted to take her back there before she got too far along with her pregnancy. He'd have to ask her doctor about traveling.

Matt kneaded the sore muscles in her shoulders and then her lower back.

"You have the best hands," she said.

She had the best back, he thought. The best skin. The nicest curves. "We don't have to go anywhere. I'll get some takeout, and you can eat it in bed."

"No, I'm fine." She rolled over, making no effort to cover herself, finally getting over some of her shyness with him. "Besides, you said you had something planned."

"I did, but it'll keep." He put his hand on one of her breasts and kissed her softly on the lips, then let his hand drift down to where the baby was. "Skipper's still tiny."

"But growing every day."

He thought the baby stirred beneath his hand, as it often did when he touched her this way. It was the oddest feeling. Like something fluttering ever so slightly beneath her skin. Probably the baby rolling over, the doctor said. He wasn't quite sure if he could actually feel it or if he just wanted to so much. The baby would fit easily in the palm of his hand right now, probably didn't even weigh a pound. He'd been stealing Cathie's baby books and reading late at night, when she was asleep, and trying not to worry about anything.

"You're sure you're okay?"

"Fine," she said. "I'm not an invalid. I'm just pregnant. And you said you had a surprise for me."

"All right. Up. And get dressed. Nothing fancy." He'd intended to take her someplace nice for dinner, after they found baby things. But he was thinking take-out in bed sounded like a better idea.

She put on a pair of leggings and one of her new, long, loose tops. If someone looked at her at just the right angle, they'd see her tiny belly and the baby.

He drove her to the biggest and best baby store in town, having checked out places with four different women in his office. They'd had a baby boom in the last year or so.

He made her close her eyes when they got close and didn't let her open them until they were parked in front of Baby Extravaganza. She got really quiet when she realized where they were and said, "Oh, Matt," in that voice that could turn a guy to mush, and then he was afraid she was going to cry.

"Don't do that," he insisted. "I just thought it was time."

"It's so sweet."

"Cathie, I am not sweet, and if you tell anyone I am—"

She kissed him, shutting him up nicely, and then grinned at him. "This is the nicest present anyone has ever given me for Valentine's Day."

Then she'd been hanging out with really stupid

men, he decided, knowing right then and there he was going back to the jewelry store to get the necklace he'd considered. No reason he couldn't spoil her, to try to make up for all the stupid men who'd had the chance and blown it.

It wasn't like it was hard to make her happy. She was kind and generous and made everything so easy. She found joy in every day and even managed to make him laugh, and most everything in the world was better with her.

It scared him sometimes, thinking about how much better things were with her.

"Come on," he said. "Let's go. I've been warned that this place covers about five acres. I hope you have some idea of what you want. Otherwise, we might not make it out alive."

That proved to be true. How many different ways were there to make a crib? Or sheets for a baby's bed? And exactly how much stuff could one little baby need?

They kept selecting things, and he hoped the place had movers and trucks to haul it all to the house, people who wouldn't let Cathie lift a thing. They spent a fortune. Not that he cared, but she would have. He tried hard not to let her look at a price tag. She'd have been horrified.

He was doing just fine in the store until they got to the baby clothes. Cathie picked up a little pink and white thing. A pretty knit sweater and a matching cap.

"You've got to be kidding," he said. "Tell me the Skipper's going to be bigger than that when she finally gets here."

She checked the tag on the sweater. "Nope. Sorry. This is a twelve-month size."

Matt felt a little light-headed. "A year before she's even that size?"

"Maybe. Some of them grow faster. Haven't you ever been around a baby?"

"Not really." How did anyone keep something that tiny alive in this big, scary world? Something that little would have to be so vulnerable. One wrong move and...he didn't even want to think about it. Up to this point, he'd just worried about Cathie and the pregnancy. Now he had the baby to think about.

"You're not going to faint or anything, are you?" she asked.

"I have never fainted in my life."

"I guess this is not the time to tell you we need to talk about scheduling childbirth classes?"

Childbirth?

Cathie laughed. He'd heard stories. About childbirth classes and the birth itself. He'd thought, *How bad could it possibly be?* This was the twenty-first century, after all. They weren't a primitive culture. Medicine had come so far, coming up with miracles every day.

Despite all that, he'd heard it was still brutal—giving birth to a child.

He didn't want her going through anything like that, had imagined he'd just insist they gave her all kinds of drugs so nothing really hurt, and they'd somehow get the baby out. End of story.

He and Cathie skipped the clothing. She had a hand on her back as they walked to the car and admitted she thought she might have overdone it a bit. It was all he could do not to insist she call her doctor.

Instead, he took her home, picking up takeout on the way, and made her go to bed. She didn't eat much, and he thought she might be a little warm. She made fun of him for fussing and thanked him again for the baby things, telling him she couldn't wait to get started putting the baby's room together.

He decided he could do that himself. She could sit in the rocker they'd picked out and supervise.

A month later, Matt got a call early on a Sunday morning about a problem with a system in Dallas that held the financial information of a quarter of a million people. The firewalls his company had erected had held up, protecting the most sensitive information, but still, the hackers had gotten farther inside the system than they should have.

He was on a plane two hours later.

Cathie drove him to the airport, hating to see him go again. She was feeling odd again. Achy and hot, kind of like she had the flu. Except she didn't have a sore throat or a runny nose. And her back hurt.

She lazed around the house, reading a history assignment and staring at the room she'd picked out for the baby, trying to figure out exactly what color she wanted on the walls and where all the furniture would go. They'd special ordered it. It was supposed to be here any day now. She couldn't wait to see it in the room.

Later, feeling better, she worked a bit in the garden. She was on her hands and knees, trying to get a stubborn weed out from around a bush, when her back stiffened in the oddest way.

Cathie sat down on the ground rubbing at the spot

in her back. She'd never had back problems before. Must have been a muscle spasm. The things she'd read said it wasn't unusual. Pregnancy definitely strained the back.

She went back to work. By the time she was done, her back really hurt. She walked stiffly inside, got a glass of water and went upstairs to lie down on the bed, wishing Matt was here.

A few minutes later, her back did that thing again. It was so tight. Instinctively, she put a hand on her belly, over the baby. Her belly was tight, too.

Scared, she told herself to breathe, to not jump to any ridiculous conclusions. She was fine.

A moment later, she felt absolutely normal. Nothing hurt. Nothing was tight. She was just starting to relax again when, about five minutes later, it happened again. It didn't hurt. Not really. It just felt…odd. And it scared her.

But then, she had all sorts of odd aches and unusual feelings in her body these days. Like it just wasn't her own and was completely out of her control. She'd had twinges in her belly before and dull aches, which her doctor said weren't unusual at all, because the muscles were stretching and finding the strength to hold up the baby, and the baby got heavier all the time. Same with her back. She'd learned to ignore a lot of twinges. This one went away before it could scare her too badly.

She went into the bathroom to rinse off, because she'd been digging in the dirt for a while. In the shower, it happened again. Everything in her belly went tight. Cathie got out and dried off, dressed quickly, and then got in bed, thinking she had done too much and her body was letting her know it. No reason to panic. She wished she could call her mother, but they hadn't even told her parents about the baby yet, although they'd have to soon.

She talked to the baby and tried to tell it everything was fine, not to worry, that she loved it and was going to take good care of it. But those odd feelings kept repeating. They were fairly regular, and after a while, they either got harder or she got more scared, because they hurt.

There was no fooling herself anymore.

She was having contractions.

Shaking, Cathie called her doctor's emergency number and, at the prompts, keyed in her phone number. Why they couldn't just answer, she didn't understand. She wouldn't be calling if there wasn't a problem.

Things had been going so well. Too well. Everything seemed to be falling into place, just the way she'd hoped and dreamed and prayed they would. Matt looked so happy, and she'd almost forgotten the marriage wasn't for real and that this wasn't his baby she was carrying.

It was a dangerous thing—forgetting like that—but that's what she'd allowed herself to do. He was going to love her. He had to.

Dr. Adams called her back, listened to everything she had to say about the off-and-on back pain, the flu-like feeling and the contractions and said, "I think you should meet me at the hospital, so we can find out what's going on."

"My husband's out of town." Cathie closed her eyes, thinking, *please, please, please.* "Is it really bad? Does he need to come back?"

"Cathie, these things happen, and most of the time, it turns out to be nothing."

"Most of the time? I'm not going to lose this baby, am I?" she cried.

"I can't promise you that. No doctor can. But I do know with absolute certainly that getting upset at this point is not going to help your baby or you. Call your husband and tell him to come home, if that will make you feel better. But call a taxi first. I'll meet you at the hospital in thirty minutes."

She dialed directory assistance and got a taxi. Then she had to call Matt. He worried so much about her and the baby already, even when nothing was wrong. She'd thought that was so sweet and taken it as a sign that he did truly care about them. She didn't want to have to tell him this.

What if something was really wrong, and she'd sat here too long and made it even worse?

She would have said a little prayer, but she still felt guilty about being pregnant in the first place. She hadn't quite been able to bring herself to even pray. She just kept talking to the Box. A silly distinction, she knew, but that seemed easier for her now.

She kept it in her nightstand, way in the back behind her exercise clothes. She pulled it out, then ripped off a tiny strip of paper from one that held Matt's phone number at his hotel in Texas. She was thinking she might as well start out this time by writing, *Sorry, it's me again.* And God would groan and shake his head and think, *Is poor Cathie ever going to get it together?*

She scribbled down a hasty, *Please let my baby be okay,* and wanted to add, *Please let Matt be here soon,* but that seemed like asking a lot. She always worried about asking too much.

She folded up the tiny strip of paper and put it inside the Box, wondering if she should be taking some things out.

How much happiness did any one person get, anyway?

Maybe she just wanted too much.

Matt picked up the phone and just the way Cathie said his name sent chills through him. "What's wrong?"

"I think I'm having contractions. My doctor's meeting me at the hospital. Now. Can you…will you come home?"

He didn't remember much of what he said at that point. He just knew she was scared, she needed him, and he was hundreds of miles away, terrified. He had to trust an anonymous taxi driver and her doctor to take care of her and the baby until he could get there, which just felt like hell. He didn't like depending on anyone. Having to do that with Cathie and the baby while she was trying to go into labor way too early…

He wanted to hit something, and he hadn't hit anyone or anything in at least ten years. When did the world get so damned scary? He didn't remember being scared in the last ten years, either.

Matt got himself a taxi and chartered a small jet, truly grateful he had so much money he could, all the while cursing himself for ever leaving when she hadn't been feeling well.

If anything happened to this baby…

She loved it already, got the sweetest, dreamiest

look on her face when she thought she was alone and talking to the baby. It embarrassed her, when he caught her doing it, and he teased her about it. But he thought it was the sweetest thing. How much she loved that baby when it didn't even seem real yet.

Matt tried to call the hospital from the plane, but all he got was a runaround from the hospital switchboard. They couldn't find her in the computer. The nurse in the maternity ward said things were crazy, that they didn't even have rooms for all of the patients they had. Maybe that was why he couldn't find her. He'd entrusted her and the baby to a hospital that couldn't even give them a room?

He was slowly losing his mind, thinking of those damned books he'd read, all the things that could go wrong.

It was an excruciating five hours from the time he got her call until he walked onto the maternity ward like a madman, insisting that someone find his wife now. A nurse in pink scrubs with little panda bears took pity on him and took him by the arm, promising to find Cathie and take him to her.

"Let me guess," she said. "First baby?"

"Yes. Not due until July."

"Oh." Her entire demeanor changed.

She punched Cathie's name into a computer, and this time, the damned machine knew where she was. The nurse led him to a room down the hall. It was dark inside, and it was only then that he realized it was nearly midnight.

"Let's see what we've got," the nurse whispered.

She went to the chart at the end of the bed and picked it up. Matt had to stop and take a breath, then two, bracing himself before he let himself look at Cathie. She was lying in the bed, wearing a plain, blue hospital gown, sleeping on her side under a light pink blanket, the baby nothing more than a tiny impression under the blanket. Cathie's pretty, light brown hair was pulled back in a ponytail, and there were dark smudges under her eyes. She was obviously worn-out.

She had an IV in the back of her right hand and some kind of monitor around her tiny belly. He saw squiggly lines and numbers on the readout, but had no idea what they meant.

"Okay," the nurse said softly. "Looks like we have some contractions. Definitely not what we want at this point in the pregnancy. But at the last check, they weren't as strong as they had been when she came in. Ultrasound looks fine." She picked up a thin strip of paper that the monitor was spitting out and examined it. "The strip's not bad. It measures her heartbeat and the baby's and the contractions. Baby's heartbeat looks fine."

"Heartbeat?"

"Yes." She pointed to the digital readout on the monitor. "That's your baby's heartbeat."

His baby? People called it that. The doctors. The nurses. The clerks at Baby Extravaganza. He and Cathie both just smiled and let them. He couldn't imagine feeling more for this unborn child at the moment than if it had been his.

Then he noticed the digital readout on the heartbeat monitor. "One-forty? It's too fast."

"For a baby, it's perfectly normal."

"Oh. Okay." He sank into a chair by Cathie's side, still scared to touch her. "What happens now?"

"We wait and see. We have her on medication, which we'll continue and hope it stops the contractions." The nurse put her hand on his shoulder and said, "I know it's hard to do at a time like this, but the calmer your wife is, the better, okay?"

Matt nodded. He had to find a way not to let Cathie see how terrified he was.

"Dr. Adams has a delivery, but I'm sure she'll be in soon."

"Thank you," Matt said.

And then she left him alone in Cathie's room.

He tried sitting, but he was too antsy for that. Tried pacing, but the space was so small. Tried staring out the window and thought of begging, but he felt like he needed to be at Cathie's side.

He'd spent years feeling as if he were completely at the mercy of the world, and his world had been crazy. He hardly had any memory of his father, except for the fights between his parents. They screamed. They threw things, slapped each other around. Matt used to close his eyes and hide and tried to pretend nothing was happening.

Once his father was gone, his mother drank even more. Sometimes she screamed and threw things and slapped him around, until he got faster and smarter than she was. Sometimes she passed out on the floor for hours, and he'd come out from his hiding place, trying to figure out if she was dead. He'd just sit there and wait until she moved. Sometimes hours would go by, before he knew.

He took care of himself as best he could, learned not to care about anyone, not to count on anyone but himself. He took to the streets as often as he could, got angrier and stupider with every passing year, until he got caught with Cathie's mother's car.

He'd thought he was going to jail for sure. He wasn't even angry anymore, just tired and cold and hungry. What the hell? It wouldn't have been the first time, and the food sucked, but they served it right on schedule, three times a day, which was more than he could usually say for mealtime for him.

He'd gone instead to a place that looked like every throwaway kid's dream. A regular house. A big one. Old, but one people had taken care of. With a real family living in it, claiming they wanted him there.

He hadn't believed a word of it at first and decided, first chance he got, he'd take everything he could grab and run. Maybe try to steal Mary's car again.

But it turned brutally cold the day he got there, and Mary was a fabulous cook and Cathie… Cathie had walked right up to him and slipped her tiny hand into his and decided to keep him for her very own. Like he was some kind of prize. She wouldn't leave him on the fringes of anything. She'd pull him into the midst of everyone, daring them not to accept him.

He'd heard Jim and Mary talking late one night when they thought everyone was asleep, talking about how they didn't know if they'd ever be able to reach him and what they could do. Mary had said they couldn't give up on him, that Cathie would never forgive them. And they hadn't.

He'd let himself stay, but he'd been careful to never let himself count on it lasting, to never let himself forget he didn't really belong. He always told himself if they kicked him out the next day, he'd be okay.

As long as he could take care of himself, he'd be

okay. He'd been fearless in the beginning with his company, taking outrageous chances, because he hadn't quite been able to believe he'd ever have anything that good. People mistook the attitude for shrewdness and daring, but all along, he'd known it was nothing but not believing he'd ever be able to hang onto anything. Knowing that if he lost it all tomorrow, he'd be fine. He had an education, and he figured he'd always be able to find a job. He'd never live on the streets or go hungry again. No one could truly hurt a man who didn't believe in anything or expect anything.

He was more careful with the company these days, a complete turnaround from what he'd once been, because he thought now it had grown big enough and stable enough and he had enough money in the bank that he could keep it going, no matter what. His house was paid for. His car was paid for. He didn't let himself owe anyone anything, except Cathie's parents.

Until a few months ago, he would have said he was a fabulously successful man. And none of that mattered at all now.

He didn't think he'd ever been so scared in his life or felt so powerless.

Matt sat down and took Cathie's hand in his. He stared at the monitor for what felt like forever, watching every little blip of the baby's heart, willing it to keep going. As if there was anything he could do to make that happen.

Cathie finally stirred in her sleep, and he grimaced as the lines on the monitor changed in ways he didn't understand. He leaned over her, smoothing back her hair. Her eyes fluttered open. She looked confused for a moment, and then her eyes filled with tears.

"Don't," he said, easing down until they were practically cheek-to-cheek. He carefully wiped away her tears. "Don't do that. The baby's fine. See? There's Skipper's heartbeat. One-forty. Perfect, the nurse said."

Cathie turned her face into the crook of his shoulder. "I'm sorry."

He kissed the side of her forehead, wishing he could take every bit of pain and fear away. "For what?"

"For this. For everything. For pulling you away from that problem in Texas—"

"Cathie, I don't give a damn about what's going on in Texas," he said.

"And because… I guess I just did too much, and if I've hurt the baby—"

"Skip's going to be just fine." He was trying to convince himself as much as her.

"You don't know that. Even the doctor said she doesn't know that."

He fought to control his reaction to the news, glad she couldn't see his face right then. Just how bad was it?

"I thought about this happening," Cathie said, sobbing. "When I first found out I was pregnant, and I was so scared, I thought…maybe I'd just lose it. Maybe it would just go away, and I'd never have to tell anyone or make a decision about what to do. I thought all my problems would go away. How could I think that, Matt?"

"You were just scared," he said. "Besides, you

can't think a baby away. It doesn't work like that, and you know it.''

"Still…I didn't want to be pregnant.''

"And now you do.''

"I do. I want this baby so much.''

"And the baby knows that, Cathie. If Skip knows anything, it's how much you love him. It'll be okay. You'll see.''

"Ahh.'' Her entire body curled up around her belly. She grimaced, her hand clamping down on his.

"It hurts?'' he asked.

She nodded.

Oh, God. Don't do this. Matt was ready to run and find the nurse, but one of them came rushing into the room, her eyes going directly to the monitor.

"Ooh. That's a bad one, huh?''

Cathie nodded.

"What's going on?'' Matt asked.

"Her contractions are picking up.''

"Why?''

"I don't know. Cathie, listen to me. You need to calm down, okay? I know that's hard right now, but that's what your baby needs. So you lie there and breathe for me. I'm going to talk to Dr. Adams, and we'll see about getting you a higher dose of terbutalene.''

"What's that?'' Matt asked.

"The medicine that we hope will stop her contractions.''

"And what if it doesn't?''

"Let me get the doctor first,'' the nurse said, slipping away before he could catch her.

He tried to slip his hand from Cathie's, so he could go and catch the nurse, but Cathie wouldn't let him.

"Don't go," she said. "Please."

"I just want to ask the nurse something—"

"What happens if they can't stop the contractions?" she guessed.

"Yes."

"I already asked." Cathie looked heartbroken. "There's nothing. If they can't stop the contractions, and the baby comes now...it's too soon. Twenty weeks. The baby won't even have a chance."

Chapter Nine

He sat by her side all through the night, leaving only long enough to make a phone call. She had finally dozed off sometime after four in the morning, sleeping fitfully, but her eyes slid open as Matt settled by into his chair by her bedside.

"What's wrong?" she whispered.

"Nothing. I just called your parents."

"You told them about the baby?"

He nodded. "Actually, I told them the day of the wedding."

"Matt?"

"Shh. Don't worry. They were fine with it. I should have told you already, but you seemed so happy lately. I didn't want you to worry about anything." He wanted to stand between her and her baby and the entire world and make sure nothing ever hurt them again, and fool that he was, he'd actually thought he could do it.

"I was happy," she said.

"Well, so are they. They can't wait to be grandparents," he said. "Your father hardly grumbled at all, and your mother kept saying, 'A baby?' in a voice I've never heard her use before. Like you'd given her the world on a silver platter. It's been killing Mary not to say anything to you about it until you decided to tell them. But now, I thought you'd want your mother with you."

"I do," she said.

Then he'd done the right thing. At least in this.

"They'll be here soon." He leaned down and kissed her forehead. "Your father told me to give you that, and your mother made me promise not to let go of you for a second until they get here."

He already had her hand back in his. Mary had sworn it made a difference. That with everything a women went through to have a baby, as simple as it sounded, having her husband beside her, holding her hand, honestly helped. He didn't see how it possibly could, but he didn't know what else to do. So he kept hold of her hand.

But then, he remembered how he'd felt all those years ago when Cathie had taken his hand and tugged him into the midst of some family tradition or a holiday or a celebration. All those times when he'd known he didn't belong and had intended to hang back on the fringes, and she'd refused to let him.

He was surprised to find that right now, he wouldn't have let someone pry him away from her side for anything in this world. It wasn't that he'd forgotten that this baby wasn't his or that their marriage wasn't real. It was that somewhere along the way, those things had ceased to matter to him.

She mattered. The baby mattered.

Not such a surprise, he told himself. He'd always cared about Cathie, even when he hadn't cared about anyone else, not even himself. And the baby…well, any baby of Cathie's would be special.

"Did something happen while I was asleep?" Cathie asked.

"No. Why?"

"You just look… I don't know. It scared me for a minute."

"Everything's fine. The nurse comes in every now and then, but all she says is that we'll have to wait for the doctor, who should be making rounds soon."

"Thank you for coming back," she said.

"Of course I came." He sat down on the side of her bed and took her loosely in his arms. "Didn't you know I would?"

"You said it was an emergency, and you jumped on a plane. I wasn't sure…"

How could she think that? It made him furious. "I own the damned company, Cathie. I sent somebody else down there this morning. Hell, I should have done that in the first place."

"No. I promised you we wouldn't be any trouble. That we wouldn't disrupt your life—"

Disrupt his life? He was furious, and yet a part of him could only sit there and think, *What life?* He had a job, a company, and a house that had never felt like a home. He had a lot of money and a fast, expensive car and could have gone anywhere he wanted in the world and found someone willing to go with him.

But that wasn't a life.

It wasn't what he'd found with her the last few months. He'd known there had to be something wrong with that.

"What is it?" she asked.

He was saved from answering when the doctor appeared. She tapped twice, quickly and softly on the door, and without waiting for an invitation, came inside. "How are we doing this morning?"

Matt got off the bed and stepped back, out of the doctor's way, still hanging onto Cathie's hand, as Mary had told him to do. "You tell us," he said.

"Okay." She looked at the chart at the foot of the bed, then studied the strip coming out of the monitor and the monitor itself, her face unreadable. "Felt any contractions recently?"

"No," Cathie said. "But I've been dozing."

"Good. Sleep is good." The doctor uncovered Cathie's abdomen, the big belt of the baby monitor still wrapped around her, and pressed here and there on Cathie's abdomen. What in the world did that tell her? "Let's check your cervix to see if you're dilating. Dad, if you'd step out and give us a minute?"

"No," Cathie said, hanging onto him.

"Okay," the doctor said. "You're the patient."

She pulled back the sheet, and when Matt realized what she was doing, he turned his back to the doctor and watched Cathie's face. They weren't going to hurt her, were they?

"Okay," the doctor said a moment later, backing

up and straightening the sheet. "Here's what we've got."

Matt turned back around, glad that Cathie couldn't see his face at the moment, feeling a kind of desperation he thought he'd left behind years ago. He didn't do desperation anymore. He didn't care enough about anything to be desperate about it.

It scared him, feeling like this after so long. He'd forgotten what a lousy feeling it was, that he'd vowed to never, ever feel that powerless or that desperate again.

"The baby looks fine on the monitor," the doctor said. "The heartbeat is strong and steady. The ultrasound that we did last night didn't show any abnormalities. Right now, it looks like the medication has done what we needed, which is to stop the contractions. Your cervix was open just a bit, from the contractions, a few hours ago, but I think it's closing back up, which is also what we want."

"So, she's okay? And the baby's okay?" Matt asked.

"Right now, they're fine."

Right now? He needed for them to be fine for a lot longer than *right now*. He wanted things to be just peachy for them forever. Where did he go to get that kind of guarantee?

"So what happened?" Matt tried.

"The lab work showed a slight elevation in Cathie's white blood cell count and she has a slight fever, which usually means there's an infection somewhere in the body and infections can trigger something like this. Maybe that's all it was."

"Maybe?" Matt was ready to explode. They'd been here for hours, and all they got was a maybe?

"I know it's frightening," the doctor said. "But so often in cases like this, we never pinpoint exactly what caused the problem."

He took that thought and let it roll around in his head. It was simply unacceptable. "Then how do you know it's not going to happen again?"

"We don't."

Oh, he was going to hit something. Hard. As soon as he could let go of Cathie's hand and get far enough away that he didn't scare her. "So, what now?"

"I think we'd be safe sending you home, Cathie, if you have someone who can stay with you for the next forty-eight hours or so?"

"I'll stay with her," Matt said.

"Okay." The doctor gave him a gentle smile and put her hand on his arm. Did she know how much he needed to hit something? "We'll continue the medication we're giving her here and add some antibiotics. Hopefully we can clear up the infection and with some bed rest, we'll keep the contractions from coming back."

"That's it?" *Wait? Hope?*

He wasn't good at waiting, and he'd never gotten very far on anything as flimsy as hope.

"Sorry. I wish there weren't so many uncertainties to having a baby. I'm afraid that's just the way it is."

And it sucked. That was it. It truly sucked. How did so many people get through this? Tons of them, year after year? All those kids in the world…all their parents lived through uncertainties like this?

"So, when will we know the baby's going to be okay?" Matt asked.

The doctor frowned. "I was going to say when it's born healthy, but then you have a whole host of other things to worry about. Like keeping them safe and healthy. I'm not sure parents ever truly relax. My son just got his driver's license, and he terrifies me every single day."

As reassurances went, that sucked, too. So every damned thing about this was terrifying? Matt barely managed not to say, *So why does anybody ever do it? Why do they become parents?* He didn't think that would go over well with the doctor or with Cathie. It sure didn't sit well with him.

"Cathie, I'm going to send a nurse in to unhook the monitors and take out your IV. Why don't you get dressed while Matt and I will take care of the discharge papers?"

"Okay. Thank you."

Matt squeezed her hand and waited. He'd made a promise.

"I can get dressed all by myself," Cathie said. "And I can see that you have at least a dozen more questions for the doctor. Go ahead. I'll be right here."

He followed the doctor around the corner and into the hall. Before she could say anything, he said, "I want her and this baby to have absolutely everything they need. If it's a question of money, it's not a problem. Not at all."

"It's not," the doctor said. "Unfortunately, you can't buy yourself a healthy baby. At least, not legally and not through any kind of medicine we can provide in this day and age. Sometimes, things just go wrong.

But the thing you need to realize, is that the vast majority of the time, everything is fine. Cathie is young and healthy and fit. She doesn't have any risk factors to indicate she shouldn't have an absolutely normal pregnancy and a healthy baby.''

"But she's not having a normal pregnancy.''

"She may have one that's absolutely normal from this point on. Try not to go borrowing trouble, okay?''

He didn't know if he could do that. He'd been ready for trouble his entire life and more often than not, it had found him.

"Take her home. Get some rest. I want to see her in forty-eight hours, sooner if anything unusual happens.''

Matt took her home and put her to bed, fussing over her and staying right by her side. It was sweet, and it made her tear up a bit, which worried him all over again. But she blamed it on being tired and worried and the fact that the doctor said the medicine that would hopefully keep her from having any more contractions often made women jittery and all out-of-sorts.

The doctor gave Cathie a few pills to help her sleep, too, swearing it would not hurt the baby and that she needed the rest. Cathie took them.

When she woke up, her mother was sitting by her side.

"Oh, Mom.'' Two words, and she was in her mother's arms.

"Shh. It's all right, my darling.''

They held each other for a long time, and when Cathie finally let go, she saw that her mother had a beautiful smile on her face.

"A baby," she said, just like Matt said she had. "I can't believe there's going to be a baby. I've been about to bust, I'm so excited, and you didn't even tell me."

"I'm sorry. I was afraid you'd be upset. Or that Daddy would be."

"Your father may be more excited than I am," her mother confessed.

"Still, I know it's not...I know we should have—"

"Yes, you know. And I know you know. But...these things happen, my darling. You're certainly not the first, and the important thing is that you and Matt are together, and you love him, and you're going to have a baby. And babies are wonderful."

"I do love him," she said. "And I love this baby so much, and Matt's been wonderful."

"Of course, he has. I know he'll take good care of you both. I never doubted that for a moment. Neither did your father. Now, tell me about this baby? Matt said you wouldn't let the doctor tell you if it's a boy or a girl?"

"No."

"I never did, either. Couldn't stand to spoil the surprise."

"It's due in July," Cathie said. "Matt took me out on Valentine's Day and we bought out the store, getting things for the baby's room, and I've been trying to figure out what color I want to paint the nursery."

"Well, figure it out soon, and your father and I will do that while we're here."

"I'm so glad you're here," she said.

"So am I, darling. So am I. I get to spoil this baby monstrously, don't I?"

"Yes."

"Your father's already wanting to fix up a nursery of our own at the house. It's the cutest thing. He has all sorts of plans. He may turn out to be worse than I am. He was gone so much of the time when you and your brothers were little."

He had been, but she'd always known he loved her, that if she ever needed him, he'd be there. He'd been a wonderful father, and she wanted to believe Matt could be, too. She'd wanted to believe everything would be just fine, but she felt like her pretty little illusion had just shattered at her feet.

"Guess I forgot to tell you that marriage can be terrifying," Cathie's father said.

"No, you didn't mention that part," Matt said.

They were sitting in near darkness in the family room, which Cathie had made to look like a family actually lived there. Matt was sipping a Scotch, and Jim, surprisingly, was having one, too.

"And kids? God have mercy, kids are even more terrifying."

"Just what I need to hear, Jim."

"But they're miracles, too. And the most precious gifts. You end up being thankful, despite the terror, because they will bring you so much joy. They'll fill up your life. Make it worth living. You'll see after a while that the other things tend to fall away, and the only things that really matter in life are the people you love and the ones who love you."

"You're telling me a man has to be terrified on a regular basis to be happy? That is the screwiest thing

I've ever heard, and I always thought you were such a smart man."

"Sorry. It's just that, I've been where you are now. I've been there so many times, but I don't think you have. Because I'm not sure you've ever let yourself love anyone but my daughter and now this baby. But it's all pretty new to you, and that first hit of terror at the thought of losing someone you love…well, men do stupid things, Matt."

"I did enough stupid things as a teenager to last me a lifetime. I'm not going to do anything like that again."

"I hope not," Jim said.

Curiosity getting the better of him, Matt asked, "What did you think I was going to do?"

"I don't know. Maybe decide that loving someone wasn't worth the feeling you get when you think you might lose them. I met Mary when I was seventeen and fell for her so hard, I never even looked at another woman. Thought everything was going to be smooth sailing from then on. We were all at the beach one weekend. Her family used to vacation with mine, and she got sick. Some stomach thing. We were sure she'd be fine. Turned out to be her appendix. We finally took her to the emergency room, and the doctor took one look at her and started yelling that they had to get her into the operating room, right then. It burst before they could cut it out of her, and she was so sick, it was three days before she even knew who I was."

"I never heard that story," Matt said, thinking every damned thing the man said just made it worse.

"It wasn't my finest hour. I sat by her bed until we knew she was going to be okay, and then two weeks after she came home, I made up some stupid lie about not wanting to be tied down and broke up with her. Broke her heart. Mine, too. But I thought I was better off never loving anyone that way. It was too much. Too big. Too scary. Lucky for me, it didn't take me that long to realize I was dead wrong, and that she might scare me half to death at times, but it didn't matter. Because she was my life. The only one I wanted. The only woman I'd ever love.''

Matt just sat there. What could he say? The difference was, he didn't love Cathie. But he sure as hell couldn't say that to her father. Not loving her wasn't exactly much comfort at the moment. It was hard enough, just caring about her and the baby as much as he did, and thinking something might happen to them.

''One thing. Women are a lot stronger than we realize,'' Jim said. ''So much stronger than we are. Pain, sadness, tears, heartache…they'll amaze you. They just keep going. I thought I was going to punch out the jerk who delivered Brett.''

''Really?'' Matt said.

''Oh, yeah. Mary was hurting so bad at the end. It started in her back, and she didn't realize she was actually in labor. By the time she did, we made this mad rush to the hospital. They said it was too late to give her anything at that point. Men stayed outside back then, pacing in the waiting room. But I was close enough that I could hear her and—'' Jim broke off. ''It was bad. Looking at her the next day, with that baby in her arms…I was thinking there was no way we were ever doing that again. She sat there and fussed over Brett, smelling him and singing him little songs and touching his cheeks, counting his toes. They forget, Matt. It's hell, and they tough it out and then they forget. What I'm trying to say is…it gets bad sometimes. But the good far outweighs the bad. Try to remember that, okay?''

''I'll try,'' he agreed, a lie if he ever heard one.

He felt raw, like someone had peeled back his skin or just ripped open his body and exposed his soul.

A man couldn't live like this, could he?

Surely no sane man would.

He let Jim ramble on, trying to nod and say something at the appropriate times. Later that night, Mary came downstairs to tell him she was going to bed, that Cathie was awake and asking for him.

He went upstairs, to the bed where they'd known so much pleasure. Already, it was hard to remember what life had been like without her here, and when he was on the road, he just never slept the way he used to. He was always reaching for her, and he didn't like it when she wasn't there.

He walked into the dimly lit room and sat down on the bed, taking her hand. Her eyes fluttered open. They glistened with tears, and she looked so sad. ''Come to bed and hold me, Matt.''

So he did. He stripped off his clothes and carefully settled in beside her, lying on his side and pulling her up against him. One arm was beneath her head and the other one went around her waist, his hand landing palm-flat against the baby.

He closed his eyes and felt that tiny mound, telling himself there was still life within her, and with any luck at all, there would be for four more months, and when the baby arrived, it would be just fine.

"How's Skipper tonight?" he asked, reaching hard for some of that old easiness that had been between them when they talked about the baby.

"Doing cartwheels, I think. Feel that one?"

It felt as if something rolled along beneath her skin in a wave. "Yeah. Skip feels just fine."

"I told her everything was. I hope she doesn't know how scared I was."

He hoped so, too.

He lay there for a long time, holding Cathie and the baby that way, thinking life would be so much simpler if he could just keep them here, within the safety of his arms. If he could hold the baby safely inside her with nothing but his palm on her belly.

Right there, Skipper. Don't you move a muscle until I say so.

As if whatever might be controlling the universe had ever listened to him. As if anything important had ever worked out the way he wanted. He should know better by now.

He should never have asked Cathie to marry him.

Chapter Ten

Cathie stayed in bed, as ordered. Her parents left after four days passed and nothing happened. Matt hovered, afraid to go as far as the ten minutes away to his office, with her but not really with her. She knew he was scared. She was scared, too. But this was different.

It was like those times when she'd seen him earlier in the fall, after she'd started college but before she'd told him about the baby. He'd been friendly in his way, willing to do anything to help her, but maintaining a distance between them she never thought she'd be able to breech.

She thought it might just be his worrying over the baby. Honestly, he'd worried more all along than she had. He drove her to her checkup two weeks after that awful stay in the hospital, and when the doctor announced that everything seemed fine, Matt looked even more grim, if that was possible.

He took her back home and then went to his office.

Cathie told herself not to panic. She took a long, soothing bath, then called for dinner to be delivered from Matt's favorite restaurant, because he'd scold her if she dared stand on her feet long enough to cook. She did set the table in the dining room with some pretty china one of his business associates had sent them as a wedding present, and put some flowers on the table, but no candles. Nothing too remotely romantic. She knew he wasn't ready to admit he loved her, but she had to hope it was there, somewhere inside of him. He'd seemed so happy before.

He came home late and stared at what she'd done.

"Matt, it's takeout. All I did was make a phone call. My index finger is exhausted, but I think it will recover, and the baby didn't even notice I exerted myself like that."

"It's late." He frowned. "You should be in bed."

"I've been in that bed for fourteen days straight. Come and eat."

He looked so put out with her and so serious, it scared her. Did he live such a grim existence that he couldn't imagine something working out well? Like her and the baby being fine, and him being happy? Surely he expected to find some measure of happiness in his life, something that wasn't going to come from anything he could buy or own?

If she'd had the courage, she would have taken his face between her hands right then and made him look at her, while she said, *I love you, Matt. I always have. And you just have to love me and my baby back.*

But she didn't have the courage.

All of a sudden, everything—not just her baby, but

everything—seemed so impossibly fragile, like it might slip through her fingers like a handful of sand.

Matt finally sat down at the table. She did, too, couldn't have begun to say what they ate for dinner or to remember more than five words they said to each other. He told her he'd pick up the dishes, kissed her on the forehead and sent her off to bed. Alone.

It was late before he slipped into bed beside her. He lay on his back on his side of the bed, not touching her, not moving at all, for the longest time. She summoned up all her courage and rolled over, draping the side of her body over his. He lifted his arm so she could snuggle against his side, her head on his shoulder, an arm around his waist, the little bulge of the baby pressed firmly against his hip.

His chest was bare, but he had on a loose pair of pajama bottoms she hadn't seen before her parents showed up.

She breathed in the scent of him and the warm, reassuring bulk of his body beside her. She thought of the nights she'd spent like this, drowsy and not wanting to fall asleep because it was so nice to be close to him and she always worried she was here on borrowed time.

"I've missed you," she said, her hand sliding up to the middle of his chest and landing somewhere in the vicinity of his heart.

She thought the beat kicked up a little harder and faster, but couldn't be sure. She lifted her face to his, took her hand and turned his to face her and pressed her lips softly to his. He kissed her back, hungrily, just for a moment.

"The doctor said it was okay," she said, barely taking her lips from his.

He pulled back, stared down at her. "She said not to."

"That was before. A precaution. She said it's fine now."

"Cathie, it's all right. We don't have to—"

"I want to," she insisted.

He frowned.

"What?" she said. "Pregnant women aren't allowed to want sex? My book said it's perfectly normal. In fact, it said some women's sex drives are even higher than usual during pregnancy. Something about hormones."

She slid more fully against him, her hand trailing down the center of his chest, down to the waistband of his pajamas and beyond. He guessed too late where her hand was headed, groaned as his body reacted, surging against her hand.

"I don't want to hurt you. Or the baby."

"You won't," she promised, thinking that maybe this connection between them could work its magic once again. Erase the distance he seemed determined to throw up between them. Let her feel truly close to him, making her a part of him and him a part of her. Let him take her into his arms like he'd never let her go and kiss her like she was the most precious thing in the world to him. She needed that.

She straddled his body, draping herself over top of him like he was her own personal pillow. His hands went to her thighs, slipping up under her gown and sliding up to her bare bottom, pulling her into place above him. Cathie leaned over him, her hair falling to either side of his face, as they kissed hungrily, greedily.

His hands moved urgently over her body, stripping her bare and shucking his pajamas, making sure she was ready for him, which she was. It had only been two weeks, but it seemed like forever. She'd ached for him.

She nearly cried out at the welcome feel of his hands on her, how familiar they were already, how much she never wanted to give this up.

In bed, he forgot all the distance he tried so hard to maintain. She could erase all the barriers here and could believe he loved her already, and that nothing was ever going to change that.

She positioned her body over his and slowly sank down upon him.

"Easy." His whole body went tight, his hands on her hips, holding her back.

"I will," she promised, the whole world sinking down to that one pulse that seemed to beat from him into her. Her whole body throbbed around his, like she was begging him to come more fully inside of her, and with each beat, he slipped a bit deeper.

He held himself rigid beneath her, the muscles in his arms trembling as he held onto her, trying to hold back what she knew he wanted as desperately as she did. But as much as she wanted it, she found she was scared, too. Just a bit.

It seemed like she'd been scared forever. He'd been the one thing she'd clung to in all the craziness, and being with him like this was the only time she could truly relax. Time when she could let down her guard, too, and let him see how much she wanted and needed him. Time when she didn't feel alone at all, when she thought maybe she never would again.

"Oh, Matt," she cried, tears suddenly filling her eyes, as she went limp above him, her whole body sinking into his.

"What is it? What's wrong?"

"Just hold me," she said. "Please."

"I will," he promised, his mouth moving ever-so-gently over hers.

Between them, that pulse kept going. He was fully inside of her, barely moving at all, rocking just a bit, and she thought he probably meant that to be comforting as well, but it turned out to feel wonderful. A sharp, exquisite kind of pleasure in the middle of so much pain.

"I was so scared," she admitted. "I don't think I even knew how scared I was until right now. And I wanted you so much." Wanted him in every way a woman could want a man. "It all goes away when you're here, like this, with me."

"What does?" he murmured.

"How scared I am. All my doubts. All the guilt. Everything. I feel safe here with you. I forget that any kind of bad things ever happen in the world, and I think—" She broke off, just in time.

"What do you think?" he asked.

That they were meant to be together. That if they could be, everything would be fine. That they could get through anything together.

"That I don't know what I'd do without you," she settled for saying.

And then, scared of what he might say or not say or how he might feel, she moved more urgently against him. It didn't take much. She'd been so close to the edge before he'd even touched her, by just thinking about being with him again like this. He had a kind of control that had amazed her in the past. That night, he just let it all go. He pressed fully inside of her, still barely moving, just holding her close and groaning deep in his throat and kissing her tenderly.

She felt the climax rippling through his body and hers, made all the more intense by how long it had been and how close she felt to him in that moment.

Oh, she'd missed him.

He called out her name, his hands biting into her hips with the effort it cost him not to thrust hard inside of her, and she felt like she hung there on the precipice with him for ages and ages, before falling over the side into the most blissful feeling of all. Like soaring high in the air. Floating on a cloud. With Matt.

Her heart was screaming, *I love you, I love you, I love you.*

She couldn't let the words go.

Tears ran down her cheeks, and he felt them and got worried all over again, and when she'd finally reassured him that everything was fine, he fussed over her some more, drying her tears and tucking her face into his shoulder and holding her close against him.

He could be so tender with her, so kind. She felt utterly safe here, always had.

And she didn't ever want to leave him.

Cathie took it easy, going back to school over Matt's strenuous objections, because not going gave her even more time to worry, something she did not need. The baby was growing like crazy. Matt teased her about Skipper being a linebacker, claiming Skip was a perfectly good name for a big, mean football player.

She finished her finals in early May, had the house looking nothing like a model home by early June and was bored as could be in July. Matt hovered, spending fewer and fewer hours at work, cooking for her, rubbing her back, talking to the baby and trying to get Skip to stop skipping around inside of her, telling the baby that was no place for games.

It was sweet. She thought he was nervous, but she wasn't, just uncomfortable and ready to see her baby. Ready to see Matt's reaction to the baby. Her mother claimed she fell in love with each of her babies instantly, the moment she first saw them. That it was a rush of love unlike anything she'd ever felt. A fierce, overwhelming, awed kind of love.

Would Matt feel that way? Would he let himself?

She seemed to sleep all the time in early July, dozed in a lounge chair in the shade of the backyard. Matt brought his laptop out there and worked at the patio table at times, not wanting to be more than a few feet away from her.

She joked that he acted like she was the first woman in the world to ever attempt the amazing feat of giving birth.

"Women have been doing it for centuries," she argued one lazy Sunday morning in mid-July. "They did it in caves and outside in the fields, when there were no doctors, no nurses, no nothing."

He looked like he could cheerfully strangle her.

Cathie laughed and leaned back in her lounge chair. The sun was pleasantly warm on her face. Matt had half the Sunday paper, and she had the other half. It had rained overnight, and the grass was still damp, the air fresh and clean. There was a beautiful, cloudless sky overhead, and other than feeling as big as a whale, she couldn't have been happier.

Other than that and the ache in her back.

She shifted in her chair, and she must have made some kind of sound, because Matt said, "What?"

"Nothing. My back just hurts."

"It hurt last night, too."

"If you were carrying around thirty extra pounds, all of it in a ball at your belly, your back would hurt, too."

She read half the paper and then just gave up and dozed again. When she woke up the next time, her back really hurt. She rolled over onto her left side, and Matt was there, rubbing her back for her.

"Right there," she said. "Right there."

It seemed to come in spasms, easing up, tightening again, and she felt so silly later, but it took her a while to recognize it for what it was, which was labor, she thought. Honestly, it looked so much simpler in the movies or on TV. The woman just knew. She went from nothing to being doubled-over in pain. Bingo. Labor!

Cathie's was much more subtle than that. She tried, without letting Matt know what she was doing, to count the time between contractions, knowing if they got to the hospital too soon, they'd just send her back home, and Matt would have had a fit for sure. She was trying to make this as easy on him as possible.

She asked him for a drink of water, to get rid of him long enough to phone her mother and father and tell them the baby was coming and to call the doctor, who told her to try to walk as much as she could and to try not to come to the hospital until the contractions were five minutes apart.

She made it to six minutes before Matt figured out what was going on and turned nearly white with what looked like stark, deep-seated fear.

She was so surprised she forgot about everything but him for a minute. She took his face between her hands, kissed him softly and looked into his eyes. "Everything's going to be fine."

He looked like a man about to be sent into a den of lions. She just didn't understand. Her doctor told her some men were squeamish, who passed out at the first hint of pain or blood, but she felt certain Matt wasn't one of them. Some just hated hospitals, but he'd never said anything about that, either. So what was it?

He helped her inside, grabbed her suitcase and put her in the car, driving a little too fast and not saying anything on the way to the hospital, except to ask if she was okay.

"It's not bad," she thought. "Like a bad back-ache." She could do this. The breathing really helped. She hadn't thought it would, but it did.

They got to the hospital without any trouble, and although it seemed to take forever, it was only about fifteen minutes before she was settled into a room, a bright, sunny one with soothing, light blue walls.

Cathie got into a hospital gown, and Matt found some soothing music on the radio. At the nurse's suggestion, Cathie perched on the side of the bed, her feet dangling from it. When she leaned forward, her belly was practically hanging in midair, which took the pressure off her back, and Matt sat in a chair in front of her. He had his arms around her, could rub her back, and she hung onto him, her head on his shoulder.

The contractions came harder and closer together. Matt stayed right there. She could feel the tension in his body, hear the tension in his voice, but he never left her side. He kissed her cheek, pushed the hair back from her face, held her hand, talked and talked and talked when she asked him to, because it kept her mind off everything else.

From his reaction, she could have sworn each contraction hurt him more than her. She kept telling him it wasn't that bad, kept trying to convince herself of it.

The day wore on. The doctor offered her an epidural at one point, but said at the same time that her labor seemed to be progressing nicely at this point. She didn't think it would be much longer, and that there was always a risk that the epidural might slow down her contractions.

"Give it to her," Matt said. He'd gotten more autocratic by the minute. This was the man who'd built a multimillion-dollar company from the ground up from nothing and ran it very successfully.

Cathie said she was okay, for now.

Matt swore.

The doctor laughed and said, "I have a mother crowning down the hall. I'll make a deal with you—if your water hasn't broken on its own in the next hour, we'll break it, and I bet we have a baby in no time after that."

She left and Matt said, "An hour?"

"It's all right." Cathie moved back into her spot, half off the bed and draped over him. His wonderful hands found that spot in her back, and he did something with them that was pure magic.

She felt like she was running a marathon while nine months pregnant. Surely that was not a good idea. Her legs felt like jelly. So did her arms. Her whole midsection was one, big dull ache. Every now and then, it was like a giant hand squeezed her silly, pushing every bit of pressure in her body onto that one point low in her back.

She tried not to tense up and to keep breathing, to hang onto Matt.

She wondered how much worse it could possibly get, how much longer it could possibly take, whether she'd be screaming her head off like that woman next door before this was over.

Matt got chills every time the woman screamed. Cathie went from cold to hot and back to cold again. Surely it had been an hour.

With the next contraction, she broke out into a cold sweat and forgot to breathe, and it hurt so bad. Once she lost her focus like that, her body tensed up, and things hurt even more.

She cried out, finally said, "I think I want the epidural."

"Thank you, God," Matt said.

"I'll call the anesthesiologist," the nurse said, picking up the phone.

Cathie slumped into Matt's arms, the contraction over. "Is it really as good as everyone says? The epidural, I mean?"

"Honey, I've seen women fall all over the anesthesiologist when he gets one going. We've got one who's short, round, bald, gay and at least sixty, and women swear they're in love with him, as long as he keeps the medicine coming.''

Cathie smiled, exhausted but excited, too. She wanted to see her baby. "It won't be long, will it?"

"No, honey. Not long. You're doing great.'' The nurse put a hand on Matt's shoulder. "You, too, Dad. Just try to hang in there a little longer.''

His eyes met hers at the word *Dad.* They'd all been calling him that, the whole time he and Cathie had been there. He looked worried and was trying not to show it. She loved him so much, her heart ached with it. And she was going to have a baby soon.

What could be more perfect than that?

Matt was ready to kill someone.

Cathie was beyond exhaustion. They'd been here for eight hours, but it seemed more like eight hundred. Where was the damned doctor with the epidural? The nurse kept telling Matt everything was fine, but she had to be lying. This was not *fine.* It could not be normal.

He checked his watch one more time. Five minutes, and he was going out into the hall to find an anesthesiologist and drag him in here by force, if necessary. Cathie had another contraction, and he thought, if only he could do this for her, could take the pain from her, he'd gladly bear it himself to spare her this.

The idea that some people had two or four or six children seemed absolutely insane. How could anyone voluntarily go through this again and again?

He held onto her as best he could, whispering into

her ear, "You're doing great. It's almost over. Skip's turning out to be a real brat."

"Don't call my baby a brat," she said, as the contraction finally subsided.

He kissed her and threatened to sit the kid down for a little chat the moment he made an appearance in the world.

He'd thought that first time she'd ended up in the hospital was bad, but this was hell. It was like sinking into an alternate universe, where there was nothing but fear and pain, where the world narrowed down to next to nothing, him and her and this room and this stubborn, precious baby she loved so much. Time seemed to stand still, literally. He'd have dragged the hands of the clock forward himself, if that would have helped. But it seemed nothing did.

He waited out the five minutes, got Cathie through one last contraction, and was ready to go hunt down the anesthesiologist when Cathie's doctor came back.

"How are we doing?"

"It hurts," Cathie said through clenched teeth.

She didn't get out any more than that when her whole body went tight in his arms, and before he could tell her to breathe and try to relax, she screamed.

He looked down and saw a gush of clear fluid, and he wasn't really worried until it was tinged pink. Next thing he knew, blood was running down the side of the mattress and dripping onto the floor.

Chapter Eleven

Monitors in the room started shrieking. The nurse called for help, and people started running into the room, taking Cathie's now-limp body out of his arms and putting her onto the bed, working frantically.

"What is it? What's wrong?" he said, absolutely refusing to leave her side.

"She's hemorrhaging," the doctor said.

"I know that," Matt said. "Why?" And how the hell did they make it stop?

The doctor ignored him, pulled on a pair of gloves and checked Cathie and the baby. "Cathie, can you hear me? We have to get this baby out now. When your water broke, you went from eight centimeters to being fully dilated, just like that. The baby's right there. If you can push, do it now. If not, we need to do a C-section now. Can you push?"

Cathie looked dazed, not quite all there. The nurse got on one side of her and lifted her up into a half-sitting position, and Matt had her by the other side. Two other nurses had her legs, so that she was curled up into a ball around the baby.

Matt glared at the doctor and mouthed a question. "Why aren't you doing the damned C-section?"

"If this works, it'll be faster."

And they needed to get the baby out. He got it. Things were much worse than he thought. The alarms on the monitors were still screeching. There was so much blood. He wanted to scream, but there was no time, and Cathie needed him.

"Push, Cathie. Come on, push," the doctor told her, then turned to her side and told the nurse, "Make sure we have an OR ready."

Oh, God.

"Don't you dare let anything happen to my wife," he said.

The doctor ignored him and talked to Cathie, who was trying to do as the doctor asked. "Come on. Just a little bit more. The head is right here. A pretty, bald head. Come on."

Matt stood there, holding Cathie up. Her hair was damp with sweat, her entire body shaking and weak. All he could do was hold her and whisper in her ear. "You can do it, Cath. I know you can."

"It hurts so much," she cried, and he wanted to kill someone all over again.

"Okay. Good. Good. Come on. There! We've got the head out," the doctor said. "Try to relax. We'll ease the shoulders out together, and then the hard part's done. Breathe. Breathe again. Try to relax. Let me do most of the work here.''

Cathie groaned, and Matt heard a wet, whishing sound. The baby was out, but Cathie slumped over against Matt, her head rolling to the side.

He had a hard time remembering what happened then. He heard the baby cry, and someone took the baby to a corner of the room where three people worked over the baby, which left three of them with Cathie.

"Get out," the doctor said, as they pumped drugs into her and worked frantically, he assumed, to stop the bleeding.

"No." He stayed by her side, held her cold hand and leaned over her absolutely still body, his forehead touching hers, while he willed her to be okay. When that didn't seem to be working, he prayed. He didn't think God had ever listened to him, but maybe, since this was for Cathie, he would.

Two more people came running into the room. The crowd around the bed thickened.

"Matt, get out so we can have room to work," Dr. Adams said.

And then the fact that they were all but shoving him aside registered. There was only so much room around the bed, and all he could do was hold her hand, which wasn't much good to her now.

Dammit.

He dropped her hand and backed away from the bed. The monitors were still shrieking. He heard the doctor say, "Get a crash cart in here, just in case," and then he thought his legs were going to give out, and he'd surely be in the way then.

He backed out of the room. With his back pressed to the wall just outside her door, he sank down to the floor, elbows on his knees, his head falling forward as he curled into a miserable ball.

He used to do this when his mother was drunk, when he was three or four. He'd hide in a corner and try to make himself as tiny as possible, and hope she couldn't find him, because she got mean when she was drunk. He hadn't thought about that in years, hadn't felt anything remotely close to powerless in ages. Until Cathie came crashing back into his life.

Please, God, let her be all right.

He heard footsteps and the rumble of a cart. Crash cart. In case her heart stopped beating.

His own was thundering. Could he will hers to go on? Could he lend her some of the strength and the speed of his, to keep her going? She was just having a baby. Millions of women had babies every year. Nothing like this was supposed to go wrong, and the real hell of it for him was that he couldn't do anything for her. A man, like a boy, was completely powerless in some situations, and this was one of them.

He hated it.

He sat there trying not to scream or beat his fists against a wall. They'd kick him out for sure if he did, and then he'd really go nuts.

It seemed like he waited forever.

People started slowly coming out of the room. He kept his head down, watching nothing but their feet. No one said a word to him. He imagined them leaving the bad news to the doctor to deliver. He'd sue her. He'd sue the hospital. He'd ruin them and make sure they never did this to anyone again. At least, he could do that.

Someone came out and leaned over him, a hand resting gently on his back. He couldn't even breathe. Finally, a woman said, "We got the bleeding stopped, didn't need the crash cart, thank goodness."

Matt's breath left his body in a rush, and then he had to remind himself to draw in more air so he could ask, "She's all right?"

"She will be."

He nodded, still sitting there on the floor. He didn't think he could get up. And then he got mad all over again. "What the hell happened?"

"It looked like the placenta began separating from the uterine wall too soon. We call it a placental abruption—"

"I don't give a damn what you call it. How did it happen?"

"I don't know—"

"You don't know?" he growled, lifting his head and glaring at the doctor in her bloodstained scrubs.

"No, I don't. I wish I did, but no one really knows why these things happen. They just do. Not often, thank goodness. But sometimes, they do. We were lucky she was—"

"Lucky?" Matt nearly exploded.

"Yes, lucky it happened when she was so close to delivery, and that we could get the baby out as fast as we did. No blood flowing through the placenta means no oxygen for the baby, and without oxygen…"

Matt felt the walls and the floor start to spin, the doctor's voice trailing off.

He hadn't even thought about the baby, just about Cathie.

But, she wanted the baby so much....

"As I said, if it had to happen, we were lucky it came when we could get the baby out so quickly. The baby's heartbeat dipped, but that was it. She was crying as she came out."

"Wait a minute. She's okay?"

"She's fine," the doctor said. "She's in the nursery. Why don't you go see her?"

Matt couldn't quite take it all in. He felt like everyone was speaking a language he suddenly didn't understand.

"They're both okay?" he asked, very slowly and deliberately.

The doctor looked him right in the eye. She was sitting on the floor beside him, Matt realized. She probably knew he couldn't have stood up if his life depended on it. "They're fine," she said. "Your wife's going to be a little weak from the blood loss, and we're watching her closely to make sure her heart rate and her blood pressure stay up. She's going to be out of it for a little while, but I think she's going to be fine. And your daughter's in the nursery. I'll get one of the nurses to take you down there and introduce you to her."

His daughter?

He thought he'd gotten used to people referring to the baby as his, but saying *his daughter* seemed different somehow.

Cathie had a little girl.

"Come on," the doctor said, getting to her feet and offering him a hand up. "I can promise you that the first thing your wife will want to know, when she wakes up, is how the baby is, and you'll want to be able to tell her.''

The nurse led him by the arm to the nursery.

"This is Mr. Monroe," she said, passing him along to another nurse, as if he couldn't be trusted on his own.

"Right this way," the next one said. "We just got her all cleaned up."

Glancing around, he saw dozens of babies. They had old, wrinkled faces and tiny button noses, and were wrapped up tight like mummies, with silly hats on their heads. Some of them squirmed, trying to get loose. Some of them cried and some of them, despite the racket, were sleeping.

The nurse led him to a funny table in a corner of the room, where a baby was sprawled out naked on her back under bright lights.

She was completely bald and wrinkled and red. Tinier than he ever imagined. So delicate. Her little face all scrunched up in a big frown, her tiny hands clenched into fists and waving madly.

"Congratulations," the nurse said. "Meet your daughter."

Her eyes were huge and so deep a blue they almost looked violet. She had a dimple in the middle of her chin, and looked grumpy as could be, like she was ready to give someone pure, absolute hell. A troublemaker if he ever saw one.

"You can touch her," the nurse said. "It's okay."

He didn't think he dared.

Did she know they'd just been through a war together? That he was not very happy with her at the moment, maybe as unhappy as she was to be here? He supposed things must have been much nicer, all snug and safe inside of her mother.

Matt frowned at her, and she frowned up at him, a huge wrinkle showing up in her tiny forehead, her tiny lips puckering and curving down at the ends.

"Do you have any idea the trouble you just caused?"

He caught a glimpse out of the corner of his eye of the nurse's head whipping around, gaping at him from five feet away. He supposed most people didn't talk to newborn babies that way, but Matt was furious at this one, irrational as that may be. It wasn't her fault. He knew that. But still...she'd scared the devil out of him.

The baby made a squeaky sound, like she might be trying to clear her throat before she really let him have it. Not that she could raise much of a fuss, as scrawny as she was. Which reminded him—she'd never make a placekicker.

"I don't know who was raising hell inside your mother all these months, but it sure wasn't you." He didn't think she could fight her way out of a wet bag.

The nurse came over and took the baby's tiny wrist, which held a tiny plastic bracelet. She turned it over so he could read what was written on it. *Baby Girl Monroe.*

"We tag them the minute they come out. She's yours. Now, if you don't want her, just let us know. We can find someone who does."

Want her? Matt scowled at the nurse, thinking he

was surely close to getting himself kicked out of the nursery.

"Sorry. My wife almost...." He couldn't even say it, didn't ever want to think about it again.

"It's not the baby's fault."

"Okay." Rationally, he knew that. But he wasn't quite rational at the moment.

The nurse slipped away. He could feel her watching him from across the room, glaring at him. So was the baby. He studied her some more, remembered Cathie's father saying a man didn't truly know what it was to be frightened until he had a child.

Not that he *had* a child.

Matt would provide for her and her mother. He'd make sure they never needed a single material thing, and he could be understanding and helpful and probably even kind, once he wasn't scared half to death.

He could be stern when she needed it, could explain to her all about the hazards of adolescent boys, and maybe shield her from most of the cruelties of this world. He'd been absolutely sure at one point that he could be a better father to her than having no father at all.

But that suddenly didn't seem good enough.

He took a step back, scared all over again, wondering how in the world all of this was going to work. It hadn't sounded that hard at first. Cathie needed a husband, a name on a marriage and a birth certificate, a place to live, some money and a decent car. Someone who could lie like a pro, and owed her big time, and that was him.

But everything had started to get so complicated from that point on, and he was starting to think he'd made everything worse instead of better for her and this tiny thing stretched out before him.

The baby made a disgusted sound, a half cough, half grunt, like she knew exactly what a worm he was.

Why had they left her here naked under the lights, like they were trying to bake her or something? Father or not, he could surely save her from that. He complained to the nurse, who said something about needing to warm her up, standard procedure, baking them this way. He pointed out that her skin was all red, and the nurse said that's what color newborn babies were. She was probably going to call someone down from the psych ward to haul him off, if he didn't shut up soon.

Matt stood there and stared at the baby some more.

"I just don't know about this," he said finally.

"Fine time to think of that now," the nurse muttered behind his back, not too quietly, either.

"Can't she have some clothes and a blanket, and one of those silly pink hats?"

"She will. She'll have everything she needs. I will make sure of it."

No, that was supposed to be his job. Which he was afraid he was going to botch badly. He reached out a hand and touched the side of the baby's head with the tip of one finger. She was absolutely bald, and Cathie had such pretty hair. The baby's little nose wrinkled up. Her tiny mouth, too. One of her fists went flying wildly, and she hit herself on the nose.

"Hey," he said, grabbing her little fist and hanging onto it. She looked up at him like she thought he was the one who'd hit her. "No, this thing is attached to you. See how tiny it is? It obviously didn't come from me.''

He didn't think she believed him. She still looked all put out with him.

His chest hurt again, the way it had when those alarms started going off when Cathie started hemorrhaging. He couldn't help but notice the baby was impossibly soft. It was like touching a whisper. Her fist was maybe as big as his thumbnail.

She pulled against his hold on her hand, working herself up into a good, long howl, he feared. But at the last minute, she dragged his hand toward her mouth. Her even softer lips pressed against the side of his pinkie, and she started sucking furiously.

It felt so odd. Like being licked by a kitten, kind of, but she was a strong little thing, too.

''You are really confused.'' Matt frowned down at her again. ''I am not your mother.''

She didn't seem to care, just sucked away. He'd seen newborn kittens. She wasn't much bigger than that, and he supposed she should know right away exactly where she'd landed in this world.

''Look, your mother is…she's the best, and if you ever scare her like this again, or hurt her…'' What? What was he going to do to a baby? Lay down the law? *Like that would ever work.* ''She loves you so much already, and she's going to be a wonderful mother.''

The baby looked quite content, finally, sucking away on his finger, those striking blue eyes fixed on him like he was the only thing in her world at the moment.

He felt, in a way, as if she'd laid him bare, all the way down to his soul, with just a look.

"Don't do that to me," he whispered fiercely. "It won't work. And it's not you. It's me. I'll give you everything I can, everything I have to give. But there are some things I just can't do."

And that was the problem.

All those things she deserved that he feared he simply didn't have to give.

Cathie woke up feeling like she'd been flung around by a tornado or something. Her whole body was one big ache.

She glanced around the room. It was different from the one she was in before, when she was having...

She spotted Matt standing by the window, with his back to her. There was no light coming in the windows, which wasn't right. The last time she remembered, it had been morning, and Matt had been so worried.

She was afraid to call his name, afraid to ask him to turn around and tell her what had happened.

Her hand went to her belly. It was soft and spongy. There was no baby inside of her.

When he turned around, he looked worse than she'd ever seen him. Rumpled hair, rumpled clothes, the harshest expression on his face, eyes wild and stormy. Was that a tear on his cheek?

He looked scared. Had she ever seen Matt scared?

"Hi," he said.

She spent so long staring into his troubled eyes that it was a long time before she figured out he was holding something, a tiny bundle that was moving. Cathie sucked in a breath, and it hurt. She winced, groaned.

"Hey, take it easy," he said, coming to her side and sitting down on the edge of the bed. She went to raise herself up off the mattress, but her body felt like it weighed five times more than it ever had. Matt hit a button on the side of the bed and raised her head. "Look who came to see you."

Her head came up slowly, and as it did, she could see more and more of what he held. Inside that blanket was a baby.

Cathie started to cry. Matt was sitting close beside her, facing her, the baby cradled between them. Tentatively, she reached out and touched the baby's cheek. It was like silk, and those were tears on Matt's cheek. She brushed his away, and he brushed hers. One of his hands cupped her neck, and he kissed her cheek and then stayed close, the side of his face pressed against hers.

"The baby's okay?" she said, nearly sobbing.

"She's bossy, hungry, scrawny and bald," he said, backing away just enough that she could see him looking down at the baby, "And she's perfect."

The baby started to squirm. She made the funniest sounds, squeaking and cooing, gazing up at her with what looked like wonder and so much joy.

Cathie let her head fall to Matt's shoulder. He kissed her forehead, as she held onto him and stared at the baby and cried some more. "I was so scared for her."

"God, Cathie, I was terrified for both of you. You are *never* doing this again. Not ever. Promise me."

"What happened?" she asked.

"You were bleeding badly, and they just had to get the baby out fast. But don't think about it now. It's over. It's all over."

"But she's okay?"

"They swore to me that she is."

And he'd been scared, too. Cathie could tell.

She felt a rush of love for him that was so sweet and so pure. He'd been so good to her, and if it weren't for him, she wouldn't be here, and she would probably be trying to talk herself into giving up this baby or worrying about how in the world she'd be able to keep it, how things would ever work out.

And the baby...

Oh, she loved this baby, from her very first sight, from nothing but those pictures she'd carried of the baby in her head for so long and all the one-sided conversations and worrying and dreaming she'd done already.

Her tears fell faster, and Matt held onto them both. *Don't let us go,* Cathie thought. *Don't ever let us go.*

Cathie was out of it most of the day. Between the delivery and lack of sleep and the medication they were giving her, she dozed constantly, it seemed. She was only half-awake when the baby wanted to nurse—something she insisted on doing over the objection of her doctor and Matt. They both argued she was too tired and needed to sleep, but surely she could feed her baby.

Plus, her little girl made it easy. Cathie didn't do much more than hold her and bare a breast. They dozed together afterward. It was sweet, sleeping with the baby pressed against her, Matt standing guard over them from his spot by her bed.

She knew her mother and father were there and thrilled. Her brothers called, and she vaguely remembered speaking to them. But that was it.

She was more alert the second day. That afternoon when the baby was asleep, her parents left her and Matt alone with the doctor, who explained as gently as possible that the delivery had been more difficult than Cathie realized.

She'd thought she was simply exhausted and had gotten dizzy at the end, remembered a lot of things happening very quickly. The doctor telling her she had to push. Matt telling her she could do it. Maybe the baby's first cry. Then everything went blank.

Matt held her hand tightly as the doctor told her that she'd feared for a moment she might lose both Cathie and the baby. That the bleeding had been severe, and the placenta had partially broken away from her uterine wall, interfering with the baby's oxygen supply. Both their heart rates had dropped dramatically. Cathie hadn't been tired. She'd slipped into unconsciousness.

The doctor talked for a long time. Cathie tried to take it all in, nodding when necessary to indicate that she understood, and hanging onto Matt.

They were quiet for a long time after the doctor left. It was hard to take in. Matt held her while she cried. She kept thinking of how scared she'd been so many times to want too much. That life could only be so good, and asking for more seemed like inviting trouble. Was this her punishment for all the lies she'd told? For sleeping with another woman's husband? It was easy to forget, when she was so happy with Matt, but she'd done so much that was wrong, and wrongs didn't make rights. A woman didn't get rewarded for screwing up and then lying to her family about it.

Her mother and father came into the room, all smiles, her father carrying a huge teddy bear and an armload of flowers. Their smiles faded quickly as they saw the tears on her face, and she was suddenly so tired, she didn't think she could even tell them what had happened.

"Will you tell them?" she asked Matt.

"Sure." He kissed her cheek and pulled the covers up around her, then took her parents into the hall.

Cathie curled up into a miserable ball and tried to figure out what to do.

She could have died? Her baby could have?

And the doctor had warned her, while the complication was a rare one and they didn't really know what caused it, they did know one thing. If it happened to her once, the chances of it happening again would be much higher in any future pregnancies. Her doctor urged her to weigh that fact carefully before she considered ever getting pregnant again.

But there were dreams in her head, so many images of her and Matt and now this precious baby girl and other babies, too. Babies she would have with Matt. A big, big family of their own. A happy one.

Too much to ask?

It seemed to be.

Her mother came into her room, tears on her face. She took Cathie in her arms and the two of them cried some more.

"Oh, baby, I'm so sorry. I had no idea it had been

so serious or so scary. I thought Matt was just all shaken up after the baby was born. Your father always was, after I had each and every one of you.''

"That's what I thought, too," she cried.

"I'm so thankful you're all right. And that the baby is, too.''

"Me, too," she said miserably. Truly, she was thankful.

"This is a blow, but your baby is so precious, and she's perfect. You have her and Matt, and he loves you so much, darling—''

"Oh, Mom." She didn't have the strength to lie about anything. Not today. The price seemed too high.

"I know everyone thinks men want sons, but he loves this little girl so much already, Cathie.''

"I hope he does.''

"Of course, he does. All you have to do is take one look at them together. It's so obvious. Just like when he looks at you, and you look at him.''

"I do love him, Mom. I love him so much.''

"Then everything will be okay. You'll see.''

"No. You don't understand." It was like the weight of every lie she'd told, every mistake she'd made, was pressing down upon her, and she just couldn't do it anymore. She told her mother, "I wish Matt loved me. I'd like to believe he does, but he only married me because I was pregnant, and the baby isn't even his.''

Cathie was quiet that day, sleeping and holding the baby, not saying much of anything. Matt was dying to make her promise to never risk another pregnancy.

The doctor's warnings echoed in his head. He'd insisted on odds, because numbers were something he understood. One in eight that she'd develop the same complication again. Not bad odds, unless you were talking about risking a woman's life. Matt would have taken the risk, if it had been anything to do with business. Hell, he wouldn't have a business if he hadn't been willing to take risks like that. But with Cathie? No way.

He'd have to make her understand. Not now. It wasn't the time. But later, he'd make her promise. He'd decided to get a vasectomy, when he remembered that she wasn't supposed to stay with him, that even without the problems she'd had with this baby, any she might have in the future would not be his. So it didn't matter what he did.

Okay, he'd talk her into getting her tubes tied. Right away. He could convince her that she had to, for the sake of the baby girl she had. That would work. Cathie would do it for the baby.

And if some man came along later who didn't understand that, who wanted her to have his babies, well…to hell with him. If he understood the risks and still wanted her to do it, he was obviously a selfish jerk, and Cathie and the baby didn't need him.

Problem solved.

If she wanted more children, she could find them. He'd help her. Cathie would love them, no matter how they came to her.

Okay. He felt better.

Her mother came into the room that evening, and Cathie opened her eyes, smiling sleepily. The baby was nestled into the crook of her arm, sleeping contentedly. Matt could spend hours just sitting there staring at them both.

"Going home?" he asked Mary.

"I think I should stay, and you should go home," Mary said, coming to the side of the bed and bending over and kissing the baby's head. "You're exhausted."

"I'm fine," he insisted.

"No, Matt. Go on," Cathie said. "We'll be fine here."

"You'll have plenty of sleepless nights ahead of you, I promise," Mary said. "You should rest while you can."

Matt didn't want to go, but from the looks going back and forth between Cathie and her mother, he thought maybe Cathie had some things she wanted to talk to her mother about. Women things. Baby things. So he decided he could give them that time alone, no matter how hard it was to leave them.

"Look after them," he told Mary, kissing Cathie and the baby before he left.

Mary grinned and kissed him, too. "I will not let them out of my sight. Promise."

He ended up taking her father back to his house. They got takeout for dinner on the way, and Matt came to realize Cathie's dad had something on his mind, too. So, it was a night for serious conversation, it seemed.

Jim didn't say anything until they'd eaten and were sitting in Matt's study having a drink. He settled into a chair in the corner and finally said, "Cathie told Mary everything."

"What?"

"Everything," he repeated. "About that jackass of a professor of hers, about thinking of giving the baby up for adoption, about worrying what we'd think or that the stress would be too much for my borrowed heart. How you offered to help. All that you did.''

Stunned, Matt asked, ''Why?''

''It's just not in her to lie about anything, Matt. I can't believe she managed it for this long.''

Matt closed his eyes and took a breath. Shaking his head, he said, ''And what did you say to her?''

''I told her I loved her, and that I wished she'd come to me and Mary with this. That we would have helped her, of course. How could she think that we wouldn't?''

And then Matt got at least part of it. If Jim was mad at anyone, it was himself. ''She knew you'd help her. She just didn't want to disappoint you, and she worries about you.''

''Well, it's not supposed to be that way. I'm the one who's supposed to worry about her and protect her. When I find the jackass who did this to her—''

''I took care of him,'' Matt said.

''What did you do?''

''Put a private investigator on him. Found three other students he's talked into his bed, got statements from them, took them to the dean and got him fired from the university. Made it clear to the man that he can apply for all the teachings jobs he wants, but he won't get them. I'll make sure of it. He won't do this to anyone else.''

Jim nodded approvingly. ''Good for you, son.''

''You were afraid I was going to beat him up?'' Matt asked.

''That's what I wanted to do.''

''Me, too,'' Matt admitted.

"I'm glad you took some more time to think about it. This is more fitting," Jim said. "I want you to know, too, that I'm very glad Cathie had you to turn to. I mean, I don't think getting married was the smartest thing the two of you could have done—and just for the record, in case something like this comes up again—don't you ever make a decision like this based on whether you think I can handle something, whether it's my heart or some of those narrow-minded, sanctimonious fools I work for. They're my problem, not yours or my daughter's."

"Okay," Matt said.

"Like I said, not the smartest thing you could have done, but I'm glad you were here for her."

"I just wanted to help her," Matt said. "She wanted this baby so much, and I—"

"I know what you were trying to do, and I'll always be grateful for all you've done."

Done? As in, something he was finished doing? Suddenly, Matt wondered, now that Cathie's parents knew everything, what exactly she and the baby might need from him now? If she'd pack her things and the baby's and go home with her parents, let them take care of the two of them?

It only made sense.

If all she'd needed was the protection offered by the illusion of a marriage, he'd given it to her. The illusion had no value to the people she most cared about, because they knew the truth now.

Matt fought to keep anything of what he was feeling from showing in his face. Hell, he didn't even know what he was feeling. None of it had been real, after all. He hadn't forgotten that. He didn't think Cathie had, either. So was that it? It was done? She'd take the baby, and he'd go back to life as he'd known it before she came?

He'd always known that she would, hadn't he?

It was nothing to bring up this sense of panic inside of him.

Matt hadn't been scared of anything until he'd made her his wife.

Chapter Twelve

They named the baby Emma, after Cathie's grandmother, and brought her home from the hospital when she was four days old, when the doctor was finally ready to release Cathie.

She was still worn-out, but ready to be out of the hospital.

She settled into the bed she'd shared with Matt, and he had the baby's cradle waiting by her side of the bed. Night came and the baby was asleep. Cathie lay there waiting. Finally, she heard Matt come in, obviously trying to be quiet. He went into the bathroom, came out in his pajama bottoms and no shirt.

She saw him bend over the baby's crib and heard him kiss her forehead and then hesitate as he turned to Cathie. She slipped her hand into his and said, "It's late. Come to bed."

He stood there just long enough to worry her. She thought he was going to leave, but instead he walked around to his side of the bed and climbed in.

Cathie sighed in relief. He heard it and was afraid she was in pain, and she had a hard time convincing him she wasn't. They still hadn't talked about anything important, like what they were going to do now that she'd told her parents everything.

Well, *almost* everything.

The only secrets left were between her and Matt, not her and them.

She didn't think she had the strength to go into it right now and honestly had no idea what she'd say to him.

"Where does it hurt?" Matt rolled over towards her. Those wonderful hands of his settled against her back, working out the soreness there. "Here?"

"All over," she admitted. "But that feels good."

She was lying on her side, so he could get to all the sore spots in her poor back.

"Close your eyes and try to relax," he said. "The munchkin will be howling for her midnight snack soon."

She would. Howling was the perfect description.

"How can something this tiny make such a racket?" Matt asked.

It took a while for her to realize this wasn't a continuation of one conversation, but that some time had passed. It felt like she might have slept for all of two minutes, but actually, it had been more than two hours.

She was going to be a zombie before this baby was six weeks old.

The next thing she knew, Matt was piling pillows

against the headboard, and she managed to raise up a bit. He put the baby in her arms. Cathie barely had time to push her nightgown out of the way before the baby latched onto her breast and started sucking hard. Cathie gasped. Her daughter had an appetite like a linebacker. Cathie was sore, and would be for the first week or two, the nurse told her.

"Hey, take it easy," Matt told the baby.

Emma just sucked away.

"Listens really well, doesn't she?" he said.

He was so funny with her, talking to her like she understood everything. He claimed Emma did, that she put on an act of not understanding just so she could get her way, manipulating them like a pro already.

Cathie smiled and leaned back onto her pillows. She was happy to be back here in this bed with Matt by her side. She thought she was going to nod off for a moment, that she might drop the baby, but Matt sat down beside her, his arms around hers, around the baby, making sure they were both okay.

For a man who claimed to know nothing at all about love, he was so good to them, so protective, so tender, so kind.

He burped the baby, and Cathie coaxed her into waking up and nursing from her other breast. Matt changed her and put her back into her cradle, then came back to bed. He lay on his back and Cathie rolled over and snuggled against his side, thinking it was a sheer miracle that she'd managed to keep from telling him how much she loved him.

But if she was going to tell the truth, the biggest secret of all had to come out: that she loved him, and she'd married him partly because of the baby, but most of all, because she'd hoped he'd learn to love her in return.

She just let it go. A week went by. Then two. Emma was a good baby. All she really wanted to do was eat, sleep and try to talk. Matt was convinced that she thought she was talking, and that everyone else was just stupid for not understanding the little squeaks and grunts she made. He said she was the bossiest female he'd ever met and that things were only going to get worse once she started communicating in English.

He obviously adored her, and Cathie thought the baby adored him, too.

Just love her, Matt. Open up your heart and love her.

He hardly went into the office at all anymore. He claimed there was nothing that important going on there. He moved his laptop into the bedroom next door and between that, his modem, his fax machine and his phone, he took care of what he had to and let the rest slide. He even had people coming to the house for meetings.

The baby had started fussing in the midst of one of them, and he'd grabbed her and taken her downstairs, claiming computer system security discussions were sure to put her to sleep. It did. Cathie had gone downstairs in a pair of sweats with her hair in a ponytail and saw him standing in the middle of the family room, the sleeping baby propped up on his shoulder, as Matt conducted his meeting from there. It had been the most adorable thing.

Another week went by. Before she knew it, she was at her six-week checkup and the doctor was telling her that physically, she was fine, then asking what she planned to do about birth control.

"What?"

The doctor laughed. "Six weeks. Husbands tend to count down to this point."

"Oh," Cathie said. Sex. She was talking about sex.

"Last thing on your mind?" the doctor said.

"Well…" She remembered sex. Remembered that she liked it very much, and it sounded fine now, in an abstract sort of way. The thought of actually doing it…her whole body winced.

"I get that look a lot from new moms." The doctor laughed and handed her some condoms. "Remember, I didn't say you had to do anything. Just know that anytime you feel up to it, it's fine. But be careful."

Cathie thanked her and left.

Matt and the baby were waiting for her in the reception area. Matt had four women crowded around him admiring either him or the baby. It was the same everywhere they went. Cathie couldn't blame the women. There was something about a big, strong, gorgeous man and a little baby that absolutely snared women. Especially seeing all the strength of the man turn into something so tender with the baby. Who'd have thought that tenderness could be so attractive?

Okay, Matt looked great at whatever he did, and she'd thought she knew and loved everything about him already, but she'd been wrong. Seeing him with the baby, she fell more and more in love every day.

He could be a wonderful father, if he let himself. And a wonderful husband, if he wanted to go on being her husband.

He looked up and spotted her, managed to disperse

his and Emma's admirers and was by her side a moment later, looking worried. "You okay?"

Cathie nodded. "Fine."

"Tired?"

"How can I be tired? All I did was get up and get dressed and let you drive me to the doctor's office."

"But you are, aren't you?"

"Yes," she admitted, thinking that he babied her as much as he did the baby. How in the world would she have done this without him? She couldn't imagine.

He took her home and insisted she go back to bed.

Cathie went into the bedroom to get out of her clothes. She put on a nightgown and was putting her slacks back in the closet when Matt walked in.

"What's that?" he asked, bending over to pick up something off the floor at his feet. "Condoms?"

Cathie closed her eyes and groaned. She'd forgotten about stuffing them into her pocket. They must have fallen out when she folded her slacks.

Matt looked completely bewildered. "Want to tell me something?"

"The doctor gave them to me."

"Why?"

"Just in case," she said, concentrating very hard on getting her slacks on a hanger.

"In case of what?"

"In case we needed one. So I won't get pregnant. She doesn't want me on the Pill while I'm breastfeeding, and she offered to talk to me about other options, but...well, it just all seemed too complicated to even think about at the moment. So, she gave me those," Cathie said. "It's been six weeks, you know."

"No, I don't." He frowned. "You mean, if we wanted to…we could?"

She nodded, and then it was all she could do not to cry.

"Can't wait, huh?" Matt said gently, taking her into his arms and holding her close.

She wrapped her arms around him, feeling truly miserable. "I'm sorry."

He kissed her forehead. She could hear the smile in his words. "It's all right, Cathie."

And then he did the nicest thing. He just hugged her. No demands. No sweet-talk. No guilt. He just held onto her, offering any kind of comfort he could give her, as generously as he gave so many things to her.

She snuggled against him, pressing closer, thinking there was absolutely no place on earth that made her feel like she did in his arms. Nowhere as safe or as comforting as this.

His body was all lean muscle and pure strength. Solid. Broad. Reassuring. Warm. Everything. She wrapped her arms more tightly against him, and for the first time in what seemed like forever when she did that, he eased himself away ever so slightly.

She backed up, stared up at him, wondering what she'd done. "What is it?"

"Nothing," he insisted.

"Matt? I know it's something," she said, and in one little shift of her weight, certain parts of her body bumped against certain parts of his, and she understood. "Oh."

He grinned sheepishly. "Nothing for you to worry about. It'll keep."

But she felt that little spark now. The one that had

been gone completely from her mind in the midst of baby exhaustion. She remembered. This wasn't just a man to stay by her side through every painful moment of childbirth and who'd fallen completely under the spell of her daughter. He was also the man who'd dazzled her in this bed for the past few months.

There had been a time when she'd been something other than a mother. Despite all the little aches and pains left in her body and the way it still didn't feel like her body again, she did remember this.

She remembered kissing him slowly and deeply and how it felt when he rolled her over onto her back, and she sank into the cloud mattress, so soft at her back, with this big, hard body stretched out on top of hers. Those sexy muscles in his arms and the power of him moving inside of her.

Her whole body started to tingle. Aches and pains faded away to nothing but a bad memory. She felt his body stirring against hers, and he leaned down and kissed her softly, slowly, deeply.

"You know, I think it's starting to come back to me," she said, pressing herself more fully against him.

"I can wait," he claimed, the gentleness of his mouth and his hands at her back in direct contrast to the tension she felt gathering in his body.

"Maybe I don't want to wait," she said, thinking she was living on borrowed time and had been for a while now. A woman had to make the most of borrowed time. "Where's the baby?"

He kissed her again. "Asleep, for the moment."

"Can we turn out the lights and close the blinds? Can we make it as dark as possible?"

He grinned against her mouth. "Why?"

"Because I don't want you to see me."

"But I like seeing you," he claimed.

"But everything's still not back the way it was. With my body, I mean. It's all kind of…I don't know. Puffy and soft."

"I like soft," he said kissing her neck.

Oh, that felt good. She really loved what he could do with his mouth on her neck. She squirmed to get closer to him, her body sinking into his. "I have missed you, Matt."

"I've missed you, too." He picked her up and carried her to bed, setting her gently on the covers and turning out the light, as she'd asked him to do, and closing the blinds.

She got under the covers and pulled them up to her chin. He grinned down at her and started tugging at her nightgown.

"Come on. You're covered," he said, pulling it over her head and throwing it into the corner of the room.

She clutched at the sheet. "My breasts are still tender."

He cupped them gently through the sheet. "Okay. Got your condom, Mrs. Monroe?"

She held up the hand that was still clutching it. He took it from her and put it on the nightstand, then started unbuttoning his shirt. He pulled it off, and it was her turn to grin.

His body was so beautiful. Hard in all the right places. Muscular in some, sleek in others. It was still hard to believe he was actually her lover or in any way her husband.

It was like he took her to another planet when he

touched her, and nothing about that had changed. It was all right there waiting for them.

She forgot what still hurt and what was still tender. He moved slowly and very deliberately with every touch, and it wasn't long before she'd practically wrapped herself around him and begged him to make love to her.

He slipped inside of her very slowly and carefully, the way he had after she'd almost gone into labor much too soon, and barely moved inside of her, rocking ever so gently back and forth. She wanted to crawl inside of him completely and never come out. To kiss him and never stop. To have him never take his hands off her.

She had tears in her eyes by the end, and she knew it took all the self-control he had to hold his body in check in the last moments. He groaned out loud and kissed her and moved against her, his big, hard body shuddering in her arms, and then she was, too. It was like falling, the easiest thing in the world, being with him this way.

He kissed her for a long time afterward, and then slipped out of bed to get rid of the condom and was back, pulling her on top of him and just hanging onto her.

"You okay?"

"Yes," she said.

"You should sleep while you can," he said, kissing her softly, and she let herself drift off in his arms.

Matt stayed there beside her, but he didn't sleep. He just wanted to be here with Cathie in his arms and the baby in her cradle beside their bed. Their cloud bed, in their bedroom, in their house.

He wondered how long she was planning to stay, how much more time they had, how much more complicated this could get before it was done.

She still hadn't said anything to him about confessing everything to her parents. He'd been waiting for a conversation that had never come. They'd brought the baby home from the hospital, and then lived in a sleep-deprived haze, when nothing else really mattered except taking care of the baby and Cathie getting her strength back.

He'd thought, *No problem.* They'd made a deal, and he'd never try to back out on his end of it. For as long as she needed him, he'd be here. Cathie and the baby would be here.

But she'd told her parents, and they'd made it clear that they would support her, no matter what. The biggest reason for their marriage was gone. She had to realize that. Matt tried not to count the days he imagined they had left, tried not to get used to living like this, because he knew it wouldn't last.

He thought about asking her to stay, because he liked having her here, and he liked the baby. He'd worry about them when they were gone, and honestly, there was no reason for them to go. Life had fallen into a pattern that felt… He thought about what word fit best. Good. Better than good. Comfortable. *Not lonely.* Maybe even happy?

She'd been happy before the baby came. He knew that. And she was happy with the baby, but with him she was… *Not unhappy.* Just not herself. Reserved, he supposed. Like she was already pulling away from him little by little each day. He'd told himself to get ready, then tried not to imagine this empty house without her and the baby. What was he going to do then?

He'd get by, he supposed. He wouldn't be afraid anymore. He wouldn't worry. Okay, he'd worry about her and the baby and if they were all right and if they needed anything. But he wouldn't be afraid, would he? Not once they were gone?

He must have dozed off, because the next thing he knew, the baby was crying. She was a voracious little thing, but checking his watch, he saw that it hadn't been that long since she'd eaten. Maybe she just wanted to explain some things to him, lay down the law, as she tended to do.

He slipped out of bed quickly, pulling on his pants and shirt, then he picked her up. "What is it this time?" he asked her. "The economy? Politics? World peace? What?"

She looked up at him with those big blue eyes that slayed him. One hand was clenched in a fist, and she was either trying to get it into her mouth to suck on it or trying to make noise. He couldn't tell which. But she just kept making her *"Ahhhhh"* sound and running her fist back and forth across her mouth. So she ended up making a noise kind of like a kid playing cowboys and Indians. She was the Indian girl, and she liked it.

"Okay," Matt said. "I'll play. But Mommy's asleep, and we should let her stay that way."

Emma very happily kept up her racket. It seemed to be enough that he was listening to her and holding her. He took her downstairs and outside. The sun had gone down, and it was the beginning of September, so the evenings were turning pleasant, and the baby liked to be outside, especially at night.

Matt stretched out in one of the big padded lounge chairs and tucked her into the crook of his arm, so she could look up at the sky. She liked that, too. Sometimes when she woke up at night and didn't want to go back to sleep, he brought her out here and let her babble on. The crickets would hum, and he'd ask her a question every now and then, so she knew he was here and listening, and she was usually content.

She was sucking on the sleeve of her sleeper now.

''Yum,'' he said, leaning over and kissing her toes through her footie pajamas, then making a noise like he was going to eat her up.

She gurgled and grinned and kicked for all she was worth. Honestly, the silliest things amused her. She wasn't as scrawny or red as she used to be. Now her cheeks were chubby and so soft. She had tiny, tiny eyelashes and the thinnest layer of fuzz-hair all over her pretty head. Her eyes were huge, her cheeks tinged with pink, and her mouth was so cute when she puckered up and started yakking.

Okay, he'd miss her like crazy.

There. He'd admitted it.

The thought of her leaving reminded him of how he'd felt sitting on the floor outside Cathie's hospital room when he didn't know if either one of them was going to make it. It was that kind of awful feeling he was trying desperately to avoid.

''Look, you need to know some things,'' he told the baby when she finally quieted and his conscience wouldn't let him leave it all unsaid. ''There's going to come a day when I'm not around anymore. Not like

I am now. And you don't need to worry or anything, because you'll always have your mom, and I told you, she's the best, baby girl. The best. And you'll have your grandparents, who are pretty special, too, and four of the biggest, toughest uncles a girl could ever have. Trust me, they will do anything in the world for you. They'll turn to mush when you so much as grin at them. So you'll be fine."

She'd stopped babbling and stopped kicking her feet. She just laid there and looked at him, so seriously all of a sudden.

"And I may not be around every day, but I won't be that far away, and if you need anything, all you have to do is call. Or get somebody to call. They all know the number. Whatever the problem is, I'll come and take care of it, okay? I'll snarl at little boys who pull your pigtails or are mean to you on the bus. I'll come watch you in the school play or your piano recital. I'll bring you outrageously expensive presents on your birthdays, and your mom won't like it at all, but she won't be able to stop me, and I already took care of school for you. College, I mean. It's done. So, we've got that out of the way. Not that you need to mention that to your mother, because she won't like that, either, but she'll get over it. Like I said, everything's going to be fine. Nothing for you to worry about, little girl. You're always going to have people around you who love you."

And hell, if she had that, she'd be just fine.

No need to worry about her. No need to panic or feel bad or anything like that.

He held back tears as he said, "I'll make sure somebody knows you like to go outside and see the stars at night, okay?''

Matt sat there fighting the urge to swear, something he was trying to give up, because of the baby. But if she was going to be gone...

He sat there, hurting like hell, and then had the oddest feeling that...

He turned around. *Yeah. There she was.* Cathie in her nightgown and a robe, something in her right hand. She had tears on her cheek.

''Does that mean you're going somewhere?'' she asked.

''No, I thought you would be.''

''Oh.'' She stiffened, and the knot in his throat clenched tighter. God, this hurt. ''I don't know what I'm doing. But, I told my mother and father everything.''

''I know, Cath.'' Her gaze locked on his, surprise and then confusion registering in her expression. So, he hadn't told her. ''Your father talked to me the day you told them.''

''Oh. I didn't know. I... You didn't say anything?''

''You didn't, either,'' he said. ''I figured you'd tell me when you were ready.''

''I'm not ready. But I'm afraid if I don't say it all now, I never will. Because it would be too easy just to stay here and let things go on the way they are.''

Summoning all his courage, he asked, ''And you don't want to do that?''

''No...'' she stammered. ''I mean, I think I have to be honest with you about everything, and then you're the one who has to decide whether you want us to stay or go.''

"Stay," he said right away, no questioning it, no reasoning it out, no trying to figure out how he'd manage to protect himself if they did. He just knew he wanted them to stay.

"Just listen to me first," she said. "You have to listen, and you have to know why I married you in the first place."

"I know why you married me."

"No, you don't," she said. "I let you think it was for the baby, and that was part of the reason, but it's not the real one. I wasn't honest with you, Matt. Just like I wasn't honest with Mom and Dad and everybody. After the doctor talked to me that day in the hospital about how scary things were at one point, my mother was trying to help me feel better. She kept talking about everything I had to be grateful for. The baby and you and how much we loved each other, and I just couldn't keep living that lie, and I promised myself I wouldn't live one with you, either. It just took me this long to find the strength to say what I have to say."

"What is it you think you have to say?"

"I was going to turn down your offer. I was going to say I couldn't lie to everyone that way and that what you were offering was too much and that you didn't owe me or my family anything. That thinking you did was like saying we didn't really care about you, when we all did. You made it about favors and money and insisted on measuring it in time. We all cared about you, as much as you'd let us," she said. "I know how hard it was for you to let us in at all, and I know you care about us in your own way, and I'm grateful for that."

"I don't want your gratitude," he said tightly.

"And I don't want any more favors from you. I don't want to have anything to do with you repaying a debt. Not for me and not for my baby, either. I want something completely different."

"What do you want, Cathie?"

"I want you to love us."

Oh, *that.* Why did it have to be *that?*

"Matt, I think you know I've always loved you," she said. "I tried so hard to forget about you and to love someone else, anyone. But it just didn't work. I love *you.* That's why I married you. I thought maybe one day, you could love me, too, and the baby. And I'm sorry I lied to you. I'm sorry I let this go on so long. I was so scared when I found out I was pregnant. I had no idea what I was going to do, and then there you were. It was like you were the answer to my prayers—"

"Cathie, I am not the answer to anyone's prayers."

"You were to mine," she insisted. "Which reminds me…"

She held something out to him.

A box.

He recognized it. Her God Box. He had one just like it, given to him by the people of her father's church. He probably still had the thing somewhere upstairs. He'd never been able to bring himself to throw it away.

"What do you want me to do with this?" he asked.

"I want you to see what's inside." She sat down on the side of his chaise and pulled out tiny scraps of paper, all folded up in tiny triangles, the way she used to fold bits of paper when she was a kid. She unfolded them one by one and handed them to him.

Thank you for sending Matt to us, printed carefully in block letters, and then, in careful schoolgirl script, *Please let Matt stay.*

The writing was much prettier, but still obviously a girl's when she'd written, *Please bring Matt back to me.* When he'd gone away to college, he supposed.

Please let Matt love me. When she was sixteen, maybe?

Please let Matt be happy. That was no longer a young girl's writing. Had she thought he was so unhappy? He tried so hard to hide it, to not even admit it to himself.

Please let me keep my baby. Let me find a way.

There were thank-you notes, from when she had the baby and the baby was okay.

And one last plea. *Please let Matt love us and ask us to stay.*

"There's no reason for you to go," he said.

"I need a reason to stay. Not just for me, but for Emma. She needs a father who'll love her completely, without any reservations or doubts, Matt. And most of the time, I think you do, but it scares you to death and you don't want to admit it. Like you're so sure it's going to get snatched away from you, the way everything was when you were a kid. I'm afraid we'll come to mean too much to you, and you'll get scared and—"

"I would never ask you to go," he said.

"I know you wouldn't. But that's not enough."

"What is this, some kind of test?" he asked. "If I figure out the right thing to say, you'll stay?"

"I just want to know how you feel."

"I feel like I always knew this would turn out badly, and that I'd hurt you. Which it looks like I've done."

"What else, Matt?"

"Like I really shouldn't have tried to steal your mother's car that day."

"So you'd never even have known me or my family?"

"I wouldn't have had a chance to hurt you this way."

"And I wouldn't have had a chance to love you. When you love someone, sometimes it hurts."

"It always hurts," he claimed, frustration and anger driving him on.

"Not always. Sometimes, it's the best feeling in the world. The only real reason to be alive. You think you're really going to get through life without loving anyone?"

"If I'm lucky, I will," he shouted. She recoiled as if he'd slapped her across the face. *Dammit.* "Cathie, if it was going to happen with anyone, it would be you. That's the truest thing I could say to you right now."

"But you still don't want to let yourself love me or Emma?"

"No."

"Because you're afraid," she claimed.

He preferred to think of it as being smart, as protecting himself. "Look, it's just me. There's something wrong with me. I don't connect with people the way you do. The way your family does. I don't open myself up, and I don't let myself depend on people. I never learned how. If anything, I learned not to. I learned that lesson very well. But it's okay.''

"No, it's not.''

"Cathie, it's my life, and this is how I'm going to live it.''

"So, this thing between the two of us was just...I don't know. A fun time? Paybacks and all that? Is that what you're telling me?''

"I wanted to help you. I wanted you to be able to keep your baby.''

"That's it? Because it felt like more to me. It's hard to imagine a man going so far as to offer to marry a woman, just as a favor or to pay back an old debt. That's really why you did it?''

"Not entirely.'' He didn't say anything for a moment, couldn't. Had he really promised to always be honest to her? Because this would likely hurt. But it was a time for honesty. He owed her that. "I did it because I wanted you. And I didn't think I'd ever have you.''

"You were the one who was ready to have a platonic marriage.''

"And that's the way it would have been—''

"If I hadn't thrown myself at you?''

He just looked at her. Finally, he said, "I wanted you, too. Very much.''

"Okay.'' She nodded, crying. "So, it was sex and paying back a debt. That's it? Because I thought you were happy. I don't know that I've ever seen you truly happy, but I thought you were. With me.''

Happy? He tried to take a true measure of the word. He knew all about fear and anger and frustration. He knew about yearning for something more, about emptiness. About the challenge of wanting to accomplish something and getting it, the satisfaction that came from hard work and success. About wanting respect. About being able to buy anything he needed or wanted. About craving order and predictability. It was the closest thing to feeling safe that he knew. He didn't know a lot about happiness.

He remembered making Cathie laugh when she was a little girl and the joy that flowed in and out of her so easily, so freely. Like she had a never-ending supply. He remembered watching her and wondering where that came from, how it would have felt inside of him.

He thought of her face when she looked down into her baby's eyes for the first time, and how it felt to sit out here under the stars with Emma babbling on about some nonsense and reaching her little hand up toward the stars, like she thought it was absolutely within her power to reach out and grab them.

He wanted her to believe she could just reach out and grab them. That she could get anything she wanted.

"You've been happy?" he asked her instead, because he thought he'd made them happy. Couldn't that be enough?

"When I forget to be scared that it might not last, yes, I've been happy."

Which was pretty much what he'd say about himself. When he forgot to be scared, it felt good. "But that's not enough for you?"

"Oh, Matt. Is it enough for you?"

"It's more than I ever thought I'd have."

"Well, you have to want more for yourself."

"No," he snapped, fear and frustration getting the better of him. "Don't tell me what I need or what I have to have. You don't know what's inside of me. Or what's best for me. I'm fine with this. Just fine."

Cathie winced at the hard tone of his voice or maybe his words, and the baby started to cry. He'd scared her, too, dammit. He closed his eyes and turned away from the heartbroken-looking woman standing in front of him, and pulled the baby closer.

"Shh," he crooned and kissed her forehead. "It's okay, Emma. I'm sorry. Don't be scared." He never, ever wanted her to be scared. Particularly because of anything he did.

Cathie walked around to face him. "I think I need to take the baby and go."

He stared at her for a long moment, unable to do or say anything. Like he'd fallen into a time warp and everything slowed to a complete stop. It was like her words absolutely knocked the breath out of him. They hurt. He couldn't breathe, was surprised he wasn't lying flat on his back on the ground from the way he felt.

"No," he said.

Cathie nodded and cried harder. "I have to."

He thought this might be as bad as the day his father walked away for the last time or the day he walked out of his mother's house when he was thirteen and decided he'd be better off on the streets than with her.

"Don't go," he said, tightening his hold on the baby.

"No more favors, Matt. The debt's paid in full. If that's all it was, it shouldn't hurt at all for you to see us go."

She reached out for the baby. He sat there with his mouth open in disbelief. Her hands closed around her daughter, who had nearly cried herself out and was hiccuping and burrowing her face into Matt's chest. He hung on for dear life, and then Emma started crying again, and he thought maybe he was hurting her, which he would never, ever let himself do. So he let go.

Cathie pulled the baby to her. "I'm sorry," she said.

Then she turned around and walked away.

He looked down at his own body, honestly surprised not to see some gaping hole where a piece of him had been. It felt like she'd taken something that was a part of him, something he needed to survive. And yet, here he was still standing, breathing, kind of. Hurting. God, it hurt.

He went inside, thinking this couldn't be happening, that it had to be a nightmare. She couldn't go. But she was in the bedroom packing the baby's things.

"I'm going to Mom and Dad's," she said, working quickly and quietly, putting little soft pink things in the baby's diaper bag. "I'll call and leave you a message when we get there, so you'll know we arrived safely."

"Cathie, it's ten o'clock at night. Go to bed. We'll talk about this in the morning."

"I can't. If I don't go now, I never will."

"It's a three-hour drive—"

"Then I'll get a hotel here in town and leave first thing in the morning."

"No," he said.

But she was through listening to him. She packed a

bag for her and the baby, carried them both to the car. He wouldn't help her. And then she came back for the baby. Matt honestly thought about grabbing them both and just not letting go. He picked up the baby and was holding her when Cathie came back into the room.

"You're breaking my heart, Matt," she said. "Do you want to break hers, too?"

"I would never—"

"When she gets older, and she looks up at you with those pretty blue eyes of hers and says, 'I love you, Daddy,' what are you going to say? Are you going to tell her love is nothing but an illusion? A lie? Or that it's just not important? Or let her think there's something wrong with her, because you don't love her?" Cathie cried. "She's already in love with you. She knows the sound of your voice and the way you smell, the way it feels to have your arms around her. She knows. And she's going to know you're not there. But it won't hurt as much as it would if we stayed, and she had even more time to love you. I'm sorry. This is my mistake, my fault. I should have known it would come down to this. I just saw a chance for you and me, and I wanted it so much, it was like I couldn't see anything else except what I wanted."

"Don't go," he said again, clinging to the baby in his arms.

She stood there looking at him, holding out her arms, until he gave the baby to her. With the saddest eyes he'd ever seen, she said, "I'm sorry, but we have to."

Cathie put the baby in the car and drove to her parents' house. When they finally got there, she let her mother carry the baby in while she stood in the driveway sobbing on her father's shoulder.

"I messed it all up," she said, then rambled on. "I was so scared. I prayed about it, and then, when Matt showed up, I got this idea that it was a sign from God, that I was supposed to be with Matt. But I think I told myself that because I wanted him so much. I've always loved him, and I thought this was our chance, that we could be together, and no one would have to know what I'd done and how stupid I was. And that everything would be okay. That one day, Matt would love me and the baby, and we'd be together and happy forever."

She finally got herself under control, sniffled one last time, and looked up at her father, who looked as calm and confident as ever.

"Cathie?"

"Hmm?"

"How do you know it's not going to work out like that?" her father asked. "I mean, just because it hasn't happened as quickly as you wanted, doesn't mean it's never going to happen."

She blinked back fresh tears, wondering if maybe she hadn't been impulsive and foolishly hopeful, just impatient. "But, he let me go tonight."

"I know. But I don't think he'll be able to do without you and the baby for long."

They'd made it to Cathie's parents' home. He knew because Cathie called. After they left, he sat up in a chair all night feeling utterly miserable, sat there until the phone rang and it was her, saying they'd made it safely.

Then he just didn't know what to do with himself. The house was like a tomb.

He finally made the mistake of collapsing on the bed he and Cathie shared and woke up reaching for her. It felt like he hadn't been asleep for five minutes, when he thought he heard the baby crying. He got up out of bed in a fog and was bending over the cradle before he realized there was no one else in the house, just him. If Emma was crying, he wouldn't hear it.

Who'd get up with her in the middle of the night and show her the stars?

He drank for two days, ignored all calls from his office, tried like hell to figure out what to do.

His life had never felt this empty. Before, he'd known he was lonely on some level, but he'd been able to push it down inside of him so that it really didn't hurt. Nothing had really hurt. He'd worked too much and made too much money and bought anything he'd wanted.

He hadn't been miserable.

Now, he wondered every minute of the day what they were doing and if they were okay, if they needed anything. But that was ridiculous. Cathie's father wouldn't let them do without anything they really needed. And they would find someone else, someone who wouldn't have any of the hang-ups he had. Someone who could love them without reservation. That's what they deserved. Cathie would thank him for this one day.

By the third day, he thought he could cheerfully die right then and there.

He hurt, and he had to wonder if it would ever go away. He sat in his big, expensive, empty house, the silence deafening. It mocked him, tormented him. He hated it here with them gone.

By the fourth day, he just didn't care anymore what it took to get them back. He just knew he had to do it.

He got in his car at four o'clock in the morning and made it to Cathie's parents' house by seven, walked up to the door and started banging on it like a madman. Mary opened the door, took one look at him and said, "Oh, Matt," like she did when she seemed to be wondering if he'd ever figure out the way the world worked, like she felt sorry for him. *Fine.*

Cathie's dad was sitting at the breakfast table. He peered over his newspaper and said, "It's about time, son."

"They're upstairs in Cathie's old room," Mary said, stepping aside and letting him in.

He took the stairs two at a time and didn't bother to knock on the door of Cathie's old room. He just barged in.

Cathie was sitting in a rocking chair in the corner, feeding the baby, and at the commotion, Emma jumped and turned her head toward the door.

Matt could swear she looked happy to see him, that she smiled and her pretty blue eyes lit up. She started waving her hand frantically and making her squeaking sound.

God, he was so happy to see them.

He crossed the room to the rocking chair, got down on his knees in front of it and reached out and touched Emma's silky soft cheek.

"How's my girl?" he asked.

She cooed and latched onto his pinkie with one of

her tiny fists, held on tight as she turned her head and happily went back to nursing.

"She missed me," he said, summoning the courage to finally look at Cathie.

"We both did," she said.

"I missed you, too," he said.

Cathie's eyes filled with tears. He cupped her cheek in his hand, reached up and gave her a soft, slow, sweet kiss, fighting the urge to say, *How could you leave me like that?* and wanting her to swear she'd never, ever do it again.

"I can't sleep in our bed," he said. "I keep waking up and reaching for you."

That seemed like the right thing to say, because she said, "I rumble around in the bed in my sleep trying to find you, too."

"I keep thinking I hear Emma crying at night, and I get up and go to her crib, but she's not there."

"Matt, I'm sorry, but—"

"I can't so much as walk into our bathroom, because it smells like you. The house looks like you, because you're the one who finally make it look like a home. I've hardly eaten. I tried playing the stereo and all the TVs just so the house wouldn't seem too empty, but it didn't work. I still knew you were gone. I haven't been to work, and I don't give a damn if I ever walk through the doors of that place again. I just want you to come home."

She looked like every word hurt, like maybe she hurt as much as he did. He hadn't thought that was possible, but he did think he was making progress. So he kept talking.

"There isn't anyone else I want in my life, Cathie.

There never has been. It's always seemed like a choice between being alone or letting myself have you. I don't know that I would have ever let myself have you, because I was so sure there was someone out there who'd be so much better for you than me. And maybe there is. I don't know. I don't care anymore. When you found out you were pregnant, I was furious that anyone would ever be so careless and so callous with you. I wanted to strangle the guy, and then it hit me that there was something else I could do. That you needed help, and I could help you. That I could finally have you with something of a clear conscience.''

"I've always wanted you, Matt. I've always needed you."

"I don't know anything about love, except what I learned about it from you and your family. Most of which I threw back in your faces. I know that, and I know why. You know why, too. To me, it's like inviting someone to hurt you. I thought I could save myself from being hurt like that. I thought I could be without you and still be okay. But I'm not, Cathie.''

He hung his head for a moment and stared at the floor. When he finally looked up at her again, he softly confessed, ''I've never been any good without you.''

He thought about what he knew, what he felt, what he did have to give her. Would it be enough?

"I don't know how I can live the rest of my life without you and Emma. I know I don't want to even try. I feel like I'm dying without the two of you, Cathie. Nothing feels right anymore. Nothing feels good. It's like, when you left, you ripped out a part of me, and I'm walking around with this gaping hole. I don't think I'll ever be able to fill it. I don't think anyone else could. The best times in my life, I've spent with you. If that's love…I don't know. It's how I feel.''

Very, very slowly, the faintest of smiles spread across her face. ''It must be love, because I know I love you, and I feel exactly the same way.''

''You got me on my knees. I'll beg,'' he said. ''Please, come back to me.''

Emma decided she was done with her breakfast. Her face whipped around, and she grinned up at Matt again and shrieked happily. Cathie lifted the baby to Matt's shoulder, slid out of the chair until she was on her knees, too, and pressed against him, his arms enveloping them both.

They were going home.

* * * * *

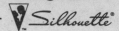

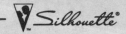

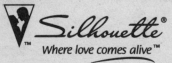

If you enjoyed what you just read,
then we've got an offer you can't resist!

Take 2 bestselling
love stories FREE!
Plus get a FREE surprise gift!

New York Times Bestselling Author

LISA JACKSON

A TWIST
OF FATE

When Kane Webster buys First Puget Bank, he knows he is buying trouble.
Someone is embezzling funds, and the evidence points to Erin O'Toole. Kane
is determined to see her incriminated—until he meets her. He didn't expect
to feel such an intense attraction to Erin—or to fall in love with her.

After her divorce, Erin has no desire to get involved with anyone—especially
not her new boss. But she can't resist Kane Webster. Before she can help it,
she's swept into a passionate affair with a man she barely knows...a man
she already loves. But when she discovers Kane's suspicions, she must
decide—can she stay with a man who suspects her of criminal intent?

"A natural talent!" —*Literary Times*

Available the first week of June 2003 wherever paperbacks are sold!

COMING NEXT MONTH